GOBLIN

BLOOD

CAEDIS KNIGHT

LONE WOLF PRESS

GOBLINS OF LAPLAND

Copyright © 2022,
Caedis Knight.
All Rights Reserved.

To the Santa daddies and the jingle lady baddies.
Stay on that naughty list!

CHAPTER ONE

Jackson Pardus, editor-in-chief of The Blood Web Chronicle and deadly feline Shifter, is looking at the neatly wrapped Christmas present on the table as if it were a ticking bomb.

"Unlike you," I say, pushing the pretty package closer to him. "It won't bite."

"It's pink," he says, screwing up his nose with mistrust. "With ribbons."

"You can play with them later."

He rolls his eyes, but I know deep down he's laughing.

Gently, he tugs at the ribbons and peels them away one at a time. I try not to focus on his strong hands and deft fingers. It's distracting how gentle he can be despite his massive force. But this joke of mine has been months in the making so I'm not about to miss the grand reveal.

Jackson holds up a pink, bedazzled collar. "Very funny."

"It's a *big* cat collar. I got it at ReallyBigCats.Com. You probably already know this, but it's very hard to find accessories for kitties your size."

Contained amusement flickers across his dark, handsome

face. He digs deeper into the box, pulling out a feather cat toy, a pack of chips labeled 'cat nip', and a t-shirt that reads *'I like big pussies and I cannot lie.'*

"Do you ever tire of cat puns?" he asks, neatly folding my gifts and placing them back in the box.

"Why would I? They are *aMEOWsing.*"

Jackson sighs. "They are tiresome, Saskia. As are you." I feel the *ping* of his lie as it hits me. Either he doesn't find me tiresome, or he likes my jokes. I kind of hope it's the latter.

I'm a Verity Witch; I hear a *ping* noise when people lie. All this pinging is why my boss hired me.

Jackson is the editor and founder of the world's largest Paranormal news outlet, The Blood Web Chronicle. The Chronicle lives hidden on the Blood Web, a handy division of the dark web where we Paranormals can look up everything from oak barrel-aged blood for the discerning Vamp, to condoms large enough for Werewolf dick. Or, you know, you could catch up on all the worldly news of the Paranormal underground.

And that's where I come in.

"Don't use your powers on me," Jackson says with a tut.

I pout. "You know I can't switch it off, my fearless leader, it's like the lobby of The Four Seasons up here. *Ring a ding ding.*" I tap my temple, indicating the relentless pinging.

I flinch as the mother at the next-door table lies to her son and Jackson raises a brow.

"Ping. Ping. PING!" I cry, imitating the shrill sound in my head. The one trick to my one trick pony.

While other Witches, like my mother and sister, can create potions, control the elements, and even control people, I can...big drum roll...tell truth from lies. I can also speak every language in the world — which isn't an uncommon talent for Verities, since different languages are another way to disguise the truth.

That's it. That's my superpower.

I can't complain, though. My Verity skills have bagged me some pretty big scoops and got me out of some deadly scrapes.

"What are you doing over Christmas?" Jackson asks.

"Hmmm, let's see." I pretend to ponder his question. "I was going to pull a Home Alone Two and see how many days I can camp out at The Plaza on a carnet of bouncing checks."

The truth is this will be the first Christmas since my sister Mikayla disappeared without a trace. I will probably be drowning my sorrows in a bottle of JD and a carton of Chinese food. Jackson knows it, but he humors me.

"This isn't the 90's. Hotels are now prepaid. And I'm afraid you do not have Kevin McCallister's level of ingenuity. You're barely a millennial. Have you even *used* a check before?"

I know he's insulting me but his British accent makes it sound like a tease. Not that I would ever admit that. I stick my tongue out instead.

"Can I get you something to drink?" he asks, rising from his seat.

"Yes! Peppermint vanilla latte, extra whipped cream, and extra sprinkles. Oh, and a gingerbread lady. Don't get the dude, the lady comes with more cookie circumference." I gesture to my rack and Jackson rolls his eyes again.

"Your sugar tolerance amazes me."

He heads towards the coffee counter and I notice all the women in the toy shop cafe watching him, along with a few men. It's kind of hard not to look at Jackson — one hulking six-foot slab of muscle rippling beneath a sharp elegant suit, with just enough tattoos peeking beneath his shirt cuff to reveal he isn't your usual Wall Street guy.

Jackson is also a massive Grinch. We don't even get to

enjoy the debauchery of an awkward Christmas office party because he banned all seasonal work events.

I mean, he's probably at the counter right now ordering himself a boring Americano when the whole place is littered with posters announcing gingerbread lattes and Black Forest hot chocolates.

I glance over at Jackson in the queue and nearly laugh out loud. I can practically hear his impatient sighs from here. He looks so out of place. Firstly, all the staff is wearing Elf hats that make a tinkling sound every time they move their heads. Which is a lot of time.

And secondly, Jackson has met and professionally collaborated with real Elves in the past. Elves that look nothing like these cute girls. I chuckle to myself at how offended by their poor imitation he must be right now.

"We could have gone to a Target," he says, resentfully placing a gingerbread lady in front of me and sliding over the cream-laden monstrosity that is my drink.

"Target's not festive enough," I say, shamelessly running a finger through the cream before popping it in my mouth. Jackson clears his throat and looks away.

"You said you need my help buying a child's present," I continue. "And *Tony's Christmas Bonanza* is...THE ULTIMATE CHRISTMAS SHOPPING EXPERIENCE." I singsong the phrase, recreating the festive pop-up shop's TV jingle. "Who's the kid you're buying stuff for anyway? Impressing a sexy single mom at Christmas, are we?"

Something somber passes across Jackson's features, but I can't quite decipher it.

"Let's go." He rises with his drink. "The gift is for my god-daughter."

"God-daughter?" I exclaim, running after him. "I didn't even know you had any friends, let alone a god-child!"

He ignores me as we pass giant garlands in red and green,

and rows of glittering Christmas trees covered in merchandise.

A pop star's rendition of *Santa Baby* rings out on the speakers as a store attendant sprays me with a gust of perfume, right in the mouth. I cough.

"Glitter watermelon bubblegum, our bestselling kid's perfume!" the attendant announces joyfully like I asked her to make me smell like a trashcan at The Body Shop.

"This?" Jackson asks, holding up a googly-eyed porcelain creature that looks like Chucky's second bride.

"OK. Let's start at the beginning." I tuck the creepy toy back on the shelf. "How old is this god-daughter of yours? And what are her interests?"

"Nine and…" Jackson scratches the back of his shaved head. "I think…ponies, maybe?"

How is Jackson able to take on all the Paranormal criminals of the underworld but doesn't know how to pick out a Christmas present for a child? Which, come to think of it, neither do I.

"I'm not an expert on kids, you know."

"I know." He examines a Polly Pocket. It's comically small in his large hands. "But you *are* an expert on Christmas. Or at least you talk about it a lot."

There's a sinking feeling in my stomach as we approach an elaborate Christmas grotto complete with a portly Santa atop his throne and yet more girls dressed as Elves.

I remember visiting Santa with Mikayla as a child on a rare trip to the UK with our mother. I remember the feel of her hand in mine as we queued, my tummy flipping with butterflies as I recited my list of things I wanted for Christmas. Things I never got, of course.

But for me, gifts were just as fun to buy as to receive. My sister used to say I was the best-ever gift buyer. It's easy to buy presents when you have the ability to discover the truth about people as quickly as I can. Maybe I can get a job as a personal shopper at Macy's if I fuck things up at the newspaper.

"How about a photo," Jackson teases, cocking his head in the direction of St.Nick.

"Alas, I'm too old to sit on Santa's lap," I sigh. Jackson's amber eyes flood with empathy. Dammit. I'm the Verity Witch around here, yet he's the one seeing right through me.

God, I miss Mikayla. I'm scared of my first Christmas without her. I've always loved this time of year so damn much, but this Christmas fills me with terror.

Not that my boss needs to know that.

My sister is the main reason I even took this reporting gig. When Jackson turned up in LA last May and offered me a role at The Blood Web Chronicle it was just after my sister had disappeared into thin Malibu air. He said I'd have access to all Para underground crime rings, and that I'd find her in no time, but so far all I've discovered is that I'm not the sleuth I thought I was. And that our Paranormal community is even more frightening than I could ever have imagined.

"Besides," I say touching a glittery parrot puppet on display. "Santa might get hard if I sit on his lap."

The empathy drains from Jackson's eyes just like I intended. Crass humor is the best weapon against pity and pain.

My boss shakes his head. "You're crude Saskia. Crude and perverse."

I wriggle my brows. "Would you have it any other way?"

Something shiny catches my eye and I bolt toward it like I'm following the Holy Grail.

"This!" I yell triumphantly, holding up the My Little Pony makeup set.

"What does makeup have to do with equestrianism?" he asks.

"Jesus, euquestrianism? You're like a thesaurus. Makeup plus ponies equals a nine-year-old's ultimate Christmas dream. *Voila.*" I pop it in his hands and he puts it in his basket.

"I'm not convinced, but I'll trust you," he says, passing a cart ladened with cinnamon rolls on the way to the checkout.

"You know nothing, Jackson Snow. *Here,*" I chuck a giant sparkly pink candy cane into his basket. "To thank me."

"How about I thank you with another assignment?" he says. "A proper *work* assignment, this time."

"Work is not a holiday gift."

"Wait until I tell you what it is."

"Jackson, I love my job, but taking down Para criminals will never be considered a lavish gift, in my book. I just want to take a few days off over the Christmas holidays and wallow in self-pity like every other single New Yorker who hates her mother."

He smiles, one that actually reaches his eyes.

"Let me assure you, this job is low on crime factor and high on Christmas spirit."

My head floods with crazy possibilities. Have the Fae glamoured all the mall Santas to do their bidding? Are Werewolves going to sabotage the Rockefeller tree lighting? Are Vamps selling blood-infused eggnog on the Blood Web?

I snicker, but Jackson already has his serious face on.

"Finland is renowned for its holiday villages. The real Christmas experience." I look up quickly and he smiles at my keen interest before taking a deep breath. "Most are lavish, money-making enterprises. Husky rides, Father Christmas visits, log cabins in the snow. You may be aware of them."

Aware of them? Of course, I am! Lapland is very, very famous. Especially amongst Christmas aficionados such as myself.

"Has Santa been kidnapped?"

Jackson makes a face at me as if he's not sure if I'm joking or not.

"Of course not, Santa doesn't…never mind."

"But, if this story is about a tourist destination, shouldn't Suzy be taking it on? She's the lifestyle writer. She did a great exposé on the Mermaid Housewives of Venice last summer."

As amazing as writing about Lapland sounds, I'm already dreading all these Christmas vibes as it is. I don't need it shoved down my throat in full 4D Technicolour glory.

"Suzy's sick," Jackson says quickly.

I hear a *ping*. Why is Jackson lying about Suzy being sick? Odd. Maybe he doesn't like her writing anymore and thinks I would do a better job. Or maybe he just wants to get rid of me and my cat puns for a week or two?

I stay silent and he continues earnestly.

"I don't think you understand, Saskia. I'm sending you on your first international mission."

My first-ever international mission!

"To Finland?" I breathe.

Jackson nods. OK, this changes everything. It's a big deal to finally be trusted at The Chronicle with an investigation abroad.

"You're spending Christmas in Lapland," he says. "At a Christmas village. I thought it may take your mind off…"

His voice trails off as we hit the end of the line and he pays.

"What am I investigating?" I ask, following him out of the store. The perfume lady sprays me again but this time I manage to duck the sickly-sweet mist.

For fuck's sake, is she serious? *Take a hint, lady!*

"We've had a tip-off that inexplicable things are happening in the oldest Christmas Village in Lapland. Their workers are being injured, property is being destroyed, and there have been a couple of strange sightings — all definitely magical. And, as you are more than aware, it never ends well when human communities are affected by our own."

I think about it.

"OK, I'll go," I say. "But on one condition. You tell me what kind of kitty Shifter you are."

Eight months in this job and my boss still won't tell me what kind of Shifter he is. I know he's a big cat of some kind, but why the secrecy?

Jackson smiles. "Counteroffer. You get to the bottom of this Lapland mystery, or you lose your job."

Damn. I guess I don't get to find out today.

"That's blackmail."

"Call it *catmail* for all I care, you're going."

"Hey! You made a cat pun!"

Jackson turns down the street, but not before I see him crack a smile.

CHAPTER TWO

The plane is landing and I press my nose against the window, suppressing a squeal of excitement at the sight of the world outside completely covered in a blanket of snow.

I was expecting Rovaniemi airport to be a cute wooden hut in the middle of a pine forest, like Santa's private runway, but as the wheels of the plane hit the ground I can see the building looks like any other small town airport. In the distance, made of glowing lights, is a large modern sculpture of prancing reindeer. Dotted around are giant fir trees twinkling through the midday dusky light.

Inside is a little less magical.

My feet slap loudly against the floor as I cross the airport, which looks like an Ikea mixed with the kid's department of a shopping mall. There are rows of cuddly toy polar bears and even a model of Santa strung up above our heads as I line up for immigration — but that's about it on the festive front.

The least they could have done is dressed the staff in Santa hats!

The immigration officer's blunt blue eyes take in my heavy duffel coat. "Reason for visit?"

I fight the urge to say *would a Christmas cookie kill ya?* Instead, I smile and say, "I'm here to meet Santa."

He gives me a cold *'I've heard this joke 20 times today'* stare. "Hotel reservation, please."

I slide over my printout and the officer examines it.

"Hullu Poro?" he says, making a face at the village's name. It means 'The Crazy Reindeer'.

I nod and he shakes his head in disbelief.

"Kuka jäisi tuohon paska paikka?" he mutters to himself in Finnish.

Who would stay in that shithole?

Clearly, the village's reputation precedes itself. Interesting...

"I would," I reply in perfect Finnish, suddenly feeling a little defensive of the unfortunate Christmas village I haven't even seen yet.

"Oh." The officer coughs nervously, caught out. He swiftly returns my documents and waves me off, wishing me a good time in Lapland.

I hail a taxi outside, huddling deeper into my coat for warmth. I never realized there were so many different shades of white. The sky is misty white, the sidewalk the same shade as the old pages in a book, the trees more blue than green, their boughs heavy with snow. The air is so cold it freezes the inside of my nose, bringing with it the scent of tree sap and winter.

"Hullu Poro," I say to the driver. He makes a face but takes my luggage anyway.

The ground, compact and hard, glimmers beneath my boots as I walk to the back of the car. Each step makes a crunching, squeaking sound.

"You know the hotel not nice?" the driver says in broken

English as we set off. The highway is strips of gray against white, pine trees flanking the road on both sides like an immense wall. "Crazy Reindeer. Not nice."

"I've heard it has some problems," I say, switching to Finnish for ease. "But I'm sure it will be just fine."

The eternal white outside is calming and despite my curiosity about where I'm heading I quickly drift off to sleep.

◆

"What, specifically, is not nice about this Christmas Village?" I ask with a yawn, picking up where I left off half an hour later.

With a sudden turn, the taxi driver exits the highway to a small road leading into the forest. "Cursed," he says.

This road hasn't even been gritted. Huge mounds of snow are piled up on either side of the car. All is so still and quiet as if the snow has muffled every sound.

"Cursed? How?"

"Blizzards, electrical problems, tourist accidents."

Just as Jackson told me. Although none of that sounds particularly Paranormal to me. I look around at the barren landscape — this isn't exactly a thriving metropolis, what's so unusual about blizzards and things breaking down in this environment?

"And who do you think cursed it?" I ask.

The driver shrugs and takes another, even wilder, turn.

"Ajatar the forest spirit, Surma our grim reaper, Joulupukki the evil Santa, take your pick!"

"Wait up. Wait up. Joulupukki isn't evil, that's just the Finnish word for Santa."

"I'm talking about the *original*. The monster. In this life, there's no shortage of those who curse. Only of those who bless."

Well, what an unexpectedly profound guy.

But seriously, forest spirits? Evil Santa? Really? I snort. I've spent the last year investigating Paranormal crimes, and even went down under with a vain surfer Merman, but I know there's no such thing as forest spirits. Unless we're talking forest Pixies — nasty things — but they live in warmer climates.

Anyway, there's definitely no evil Santa or any Santa for that matter. I did read about an Ohio Vampire mall Santa once in The Chronicle, but he was just taking evening shifts to get out of debt and got caught snacking on the job.

It's mid-afternoon and night has already fallen, speckled indigo shadows loom between the firs and birches. The trees are so heavy with snow they no longer look like trees, more like oddly-shaped mounds of icing.

'White Christmas,' plays softly on the radio. Good to know Bublé has emerged from his pre-Christmas hibernation. If the landscape didn't look so much like the opening scene of a Nordic Noir horror, I might even start to get a bit excited about spending the holidays in the land of Christmas. But all I can think about is getting out of this wilderness and into a cozy bar where they serve Baileys and ginger snaps.

"Do you really believe in an evil Santa?" I ask the stoic driver again, more out of amusement than curiosity. He squares his shoulders and huffs through his nose.

"No, I guess not."

I hear the *ping* of his lie.

"Things are different in the Arctic Circle. A little more mysterious," he elaborates. "But hey, I don't want to ruin your holiday with talk of monsters."

"Don't worry," I mumble, but the rest is too quiet for him to hear. "I'm used to monsters."

We sit in silence the rest of the way, the scenes outside

becoming a dizzying blur of white until, with a sudden screech, we jolt to a halt.

The driver curses under his breath. "That wasn't there earlier," he says, pointing at a snow drift blocking our path.

"The snow? I mean, there's no shortage of snow around here."

He shakes his head, letting out a heavy sigh and something that sounds like '*cursed*.'

"The road wasn't blocked like this a few hours ago when I drove through. It's been blocked on purpose."

I look around. There are no cars, no houses, no anything as far as the eye can see. Who and why would anyone block this road?

"What were you doing here before? Dropping more guests off?" I venture, hoping he's going to tell me where I'm heading is a popular resort despite its reputation.

"I was picking them up. They couldn't leave quick enough."

He gets out of the car and stands in front of the huge wall of snow, hands on hips as if it might move if he stares at it sternly enough. I pull down my window, the icy blast of the wind making my eyes water.

"Do you have a shovel?" I shout out.

He turns to me, his skin a pinched shade of pink. "I'm not touching that. I'm getting out of here."

"What does that mean?"

"It means you walk."

He has to be fucking joking! One look at his stern face tells me he isn't. This place clearly gives him the heebie-jeebies and he's happy to leave me with the mounds of cursed snow, to be eaten by forest spirits.

"Well, Merry Christmas to you as well," I hiss.

I step out of the taxi, my feet sinking ankle-deep into the powdery snow, my socks becoming instantly wet. The driver has already dumped my suitcase at my feet and before I have the chance to ask for directions he does a U-turn and disappears into the misty distance.

"That's zero stars on whatever the version of Finnish YELP is!!!"

Zero stars: Driver from this company talked shit about mythical creatures then dumped me to be eaten alive by zombie reindeer.

As I imagine typing out my angry review my feet sink deeper and deeper until the snow reaches my ankles and I lose my balance, toppling over into the snow.

Great!

I wipe the powder from my face and check my phone — Google Maps always has the answer. But, of course, my phone has no reception or 4G out here. This is why people get killed in forests BECAUSE THERE'S NO PHONE RECEPTION!

I put on my thick woolen hat and squint at something through the trees. In the distance, I can just make out the blurry haze of warm lights.

Grunting like an overweight snow leopard in heat, I struggle to pull my suitcase through the fluffy mounds, tripping over with each step until every inch of me is soaking wet. *Fuck this!* My feet are aching and so cold they've turned to blocks of ice.

I spot a path up ahead leading to some hazy lights in the distance. This is it! If I can find some ground that's not covered in snow, I may be able to wheel this suitcase behind me.

I run-stumble towards the path, trip over again, look up, and release a guttural warrior cry. Where the hell has the path gone? It's disappeared, only to be replaced by yet more mountains of snow.

Tears stream down my face from the biting wind, making my cheeks burn even more from the cold. Squinting into the night like a vision-impaired moth, I can't even see the lights anymore.

God, I feel pathetic!

An Elemental Witch would be able to clear a path through the snow in seconds, a Brew Witch could create a brew so strong that her body would not feel the cold, and a Touch Mage, like my mom, could simply use compulsion to make the cab driver shovel the snow away and accompany her to her front door, all while merrily singing *Deck The Halls.*

But me? All I can do is know for certain that the cabbie believes in Santa. Useless. I spit into the woods as my leg catches on an icy lump of snow and I trip over.

"Fuck you, forest Fairies!"

It's like I'm in a scene from every Christmas movie ever, when the girl has to trudge through the snow to a secluded cottage, except the main characters always look way cuter than I probably do right now. Plus, there's no Jude Law waiting for me at the end of the trail.

I stop for a breather and look back at how far I've come. But instead of a winding path cutting through the snow behind me, it's all clean and untouched as if it's been snowing heavily. It hasn't. I squint into the distance again and shudder. Something weird is definitely going on here!

The lights in the distance have grown larger and brighter. That *has* to be the village.

I pull my wooly hat down further and push forward.

CHAPTER THREE

B y the time I arrive at the gated entrance to The Crazy Reindeer, my thermals are soaked in sweat and my cheeks are raw and stinging. My makeup has probably gone full raccoon too.

A crooked Hullu Poro sign presides over the village entrance. It looks like it was once lit up, but the bulbs have all been smashed. I run my hand along a chipped sign that reads *Santa* with an arrow pointing at absolutely nothing. The curls of flaking paint crumble at my fingertips.

Cursed.

The driver's creepy words float back to me. I don't know about cursed, but this place is definitely broke with a capital B. I trudge further into the village expecting to see something wondrous, but there's just one main building and a bunch of smaller cabins. Is this it?

I stop at a wooden board where the faint remains of a painted map show visitors where to find each attraction. Light snow gathers on my eyelashes as I take a minute to get my breath back and examine the peeling signage.

It says there's a Mrs. Claus candy store, a Christmas

market, and even an ice rink. I look from the map to the village and the map again. There's no sign of any of that. Maybe all the excitement is behind the main building? Peering at the faded lettering on the board I read the site's history.

'Having passed down four generations of the same Finnish family, The Crazy Reindeer was one of the first ever Christmas villages in the world,' it says.

Well, damn.

'Founded by Mr. Iloinen in 1898, it soon became a much-loved local attraction, eventually becoming an international holiday destination in the 1950s. Since then it has opened its doors to movie stars, presidents, and thousands of children around the world who flock to our village for authentic Finnish charm and Christmas magic.'

I peer past the board. If crickets lived in the snow, I would be hearing them right now. Where is everybody? Christmas is just around the corner and the place is completely empty.

Dragging my suitcase through the last hundred feet of snow, I follow the sign to the main building — a low, one-story wooden cabin with a large hand-painted sign that reads 'Reception.'

I step inside and instantly breathe a sigh of relief. It looks exactly as I imagined. The walls are made of giant logs that appear to have been here for over a hundred years. I guess they have, judging by the cobwebs on them. The bay windows are made of dozens of tiny black steel squares of swirly thick glass, each one dusted with fine snow, old tartan curtains tied back with tatty bows.

It's turned pitch dark outside. I have no clue what the time is but that means nothing this far north in winter; night lasts forever out here.

An attempt at Christmas decorations hangs over the

entrance to the door, dried holly, and plastic berries, along with a 1950's-looking Santa statue greeting guests at the entrance. Not that there are many guests wandering about, just a few people drinking hot chocolate on rustic benches scattered with crimson and tartan throw cushions and blankets.

I notice there are no large electric lights here either. Instead, there's a large roaring log fire and the high vaulted ceiling is decorated with twinkling lights. Thick candles are dotted around the room, most of which have burned down to their quick, oozing creamy wax onto the worn wooden flooring. Everything in this place is old, worn, and tired, but I like it. It's homely.

My arms burn from having pulled my suitcase through the snow and I shake them out, my feet already beginning to thaw. A wave of tiredness makes my eyelids droop as the wintery scent of pine and baked goods envelop me — I'm already dreaming of my cozy log cabin and a hot, candlelit bath.

I step further into the foyer and notice a rocking chair in the corner with a box of wool and some knitting needles on it as if whoever was sitting there will be back any moment. So far, so *hygge*.

This is more like it!

The people drinking hot chocolate say something about needing to go home soon, they must be locals, and a minute later I'm alone in reception. Just me and the Christmas carols playing over the crackling speakers.

I wheel my bag over to the check-in desk, which is also covered in stubby candles, each one like tiny snowmen that have melted in the room's heat.

There's no one behind the desk.

Peering over the counter I notice it's littered with papers, pens, a half-eaten sandwich, and a mug of something brown.

On the wooden counter is a tiny golden bell with a sign reading 'Ring for Santa'.

I poise my hand over the bell to ring it when a breeze blows from nowhere, sending a bunch of paperwork fluttering to the floor. I turn to look at the entrance but no one has come in and the door is still closed. Strange.

I walk around the reception desk to pick up the papers, noticing each one is stamped with red text. Most of them are bills and final notices.

As I reach for the last piece of paper on the floor the mug, of what turns out to be ice-cold coffee, falls on my head, splattering my already-wet clothes and shoes.

What the flying fuck?

Jumping up I survey the room, ready to donkey-punch whoever spilled java on my thrifted 80's snowsuit but... there's no one there. A child's giggle carries across the air of the empty room.

This place gives me the creeps!

Maybe it's haunted? Maybe the local ghosts are pulling a Dickens and fucking the place up as some major life lesson for its Scrooge owners.

I've never covered a story with ghosts, it doesn't come up often. Hauntings are complex... and pretty much the only thing that freaks me out in my Paranormal world.

OK, haunted or not, I'm going to need to freaking check in! Where's a member of staff?

Ding. Ding. I take out my frustration on the teeny golden bell. I hear a strange yelp but can't see anyone. Is this someone's idea of a joke?

Sweat is already trickling down the inside of my legs. It's like my thighs went to a screening of The Family Stone and are crying.

Where the hell is the receptionist? I need dry clothes and a bath.

I ring the bell again, this time a lot louder.

If the hot chocolate locals hadn't already left, I'd have definitely scared them away, because I'm ringing this bell like a Karen summoning Santa's customer service department.

This place isn't haunted, it's just really badly managed!

I slam my hand down on the bell again, taking all my frustration out on the little gold button, again and again, until a blond man emerges from a door to my right.

Dressed like a Nordic lumberjack, he's wearing a flour-dusted apron over red and black flannel, and he's wiping his hands on a dishcloth.

Is he the chef? I can see, beyond reception, that there's some kind of restaurant. Does this place have a bar? I hope so. I could use a shot of sambuca.

"What do you want?" he grunts.

What a way to greet your guests!

"Hi, I'm checking in. My name is Saskia and I'm a reporter for *Travel Daily*, from New York," I say, flashing him one of my many fake press passes.

Obviously, I'm not going to say I'm a reporter for a Paranormal online newspaper. This guy barely looks like he can tolerate people in his own world, let alone mine.

He frowns. "*Travel Daily?*"

"Yeah, I'm doing a piece on…" I glance around and see a sign that says *The Oldest Christmas Village in Lapland*. "On Finnish artisanal tourism, specifically the old-but-trusted Lapland villages."

He's still frowning. In fact, I'm having a hard time imagining his face doing anything but.

"One minute," he grunts, stepping behind the front desk. He has to stoop to fit beneath one of the lower beams. Why do men get taller the further north they go?

He sighs and rubs his stubbly chin as he checks his filing system. Although by 'filing system' I mean reams of old-school paper and a Rolodex I've only ever seen in memes. Don't they have WiFi here?

Crap! What if there's no WiFi ?

"I don't see your reservation," he replies.

"That's impossible, I booked via carrier pigeon." I throw a pointed look at his Rolodex.

"No reservation. Can't help you," he says, missing the joke.

"My editor confirmed the booking with you yesterday. Can I speak to a member of the front desk staff?"

"I *am* the front desk staff."

"Well… Is there a reservation number I can call?"

He smiles. "Sure."

He takes his time writing down a number, then slides it across the desk. I pull out my cell and dial it while he watches me closely. What a weirdo.

The ancient rotary phone next to him rings and he picks it up.

"Reservation department."

I roll my eyes. "Seriously? You stole that joke from a movie."

"No, I didn't. I don't have a DVD player."

A DVD player?

"I didn't know this was Christmas with the fucking Flinstones."

"Flinstones?"

Right, no DVD player.

"I'm going to deal with the fact that you don't know The Flinstones later…" He cuts me off and taps the receiver at his ear, so I shout into my phone. "Just find my reservation!"

"Sorry, can't help you, we're fully booked," he says gruffly, then hangs up and walks away. Just like that.

I struggle out of my coat and throw it over my suitcase. The wooden unit on the wall behind the desk, painted with dozens of numbers, is literally full of room keys. Fully booked, my ass!

What a jerk!

I follow him into the back room behind the desk, which contains nothing but a table and more papers.

"What the hell is your problem?"

"I don't like reporters," he replies, pushing past me back to reception. From this angle, I can see there *is* a bar, but it's just an extension of the front desk.

"Well, whether I stay here or not isn't up to you. It's up to the owner."

He leans against the wooden bar. "I *am* the owner. And the receptionist. *And* the cook."

"Oh, a jackass of all trades."

He stares at me. "You think you're the first reporter to come here? Hoping to write about the plight of the last artisanal village in Lapland? How the mighty have fallen eh? You're not. We have enough problems without you sensationalizing them."

Hmmm, interesting.

It makes sense that the immigration officer and the taxi driver had both heard of this village if it was in the local newspapers.

"Calm down, I'm not here to cause any trouble. I'm just a very specific reporter who has expertise in a specific field of things. And maybe I can use my journalistic skills to help you with your problems."

"What problems?"

"*Seriously*, what problems?" I gesture at the door. "You don't even have a road." I lower my voice. "It's no secret this place is suffering from a lot of...bad luck? Let me help."

I don't tell him about my *A Christmas Carol* theory, even though the more he speaks the more I'm certain he's the perfect candidate to be lectured by ghosts on his miserable behavior. God, this guy really puts the Dick in Dickens.

He keeps staring at me, his eyes a bright crystal blue and totally unnerving. He's really not a talker.

"Look, I'm an investigative reporter and I'm good at my job," I explain. "Do you want me to solve whatever inexplicable shenanigans have been going around your corner of the world, or not?"

"A travel writer who solves inconvenient mysteries?"

"A travel writer who has a *background* in investigative reporting. I get my story and you get some answers. Winner winner, Christmas dinner." I look around at the old, tired lobby. It's obvious how grand it once was, and how much work there is to be done to bring it back to its former glory. "Looks like you need all the help you can get."

"Are you one of those hippy ladies that believe our misfortune is a curse? Or..." He lets out a wry laugh. "Something *otherworldly*. Maybe the Keiju are wreaking havoc on us. *Maybe* an Otso will emerge from the woods and pick his teeth with my bones."

All the men in this country seem to be obsessed with monsters. I know he's mocking me, thinking I'm some kook reporter who's come here to track down the forest Pixies and bear spirits that have ruined his village, but I can also tell he doesn't find the prospect as funny, or as ridiculous, as he's letting on.

"Curses, spirits, Pixies, it's all reindeer shit," he adds.

I feel the *ping* of his lie. He's more of a believer than he lets on.

"All I said was that this place was in need of some help. I didn't say anything about anything...otherworldly."

I narrow my gaze, taking in all 6 feet-something of him. He's got disheveled dark-blonde hair and a weathered look that suggests he spends time outside, maybe cutting wood, or burying food for winter. There's a sprinkle of freckles that look out of place on his grumpy, rugged face, although they do confirm my outdoorsy theory.

I glance quickly at his hands and notice that his skin is rough, and his neat nails have dough coated on them. This is a man who is used to getting his hands dirty, both inside and out.

He's staring back at me. Does he ever blink?

"Let's just say I'm one of those 'questions everything' reporter kooks," I tell him.

He finally breaks his stare and looks off towards the bar. "I doubt you can help."

"Well, that's a risk you need to take. What do you have to lose?"

"Everything," he spits back.

Oh. Interesting.

"Listen, whatever your name is," I say. "Your holiday village is fucked. You say you're fully booked but I can see you have no guests, you certainly have no staff, and even security at the airport thinks you're a joke. Let me help you or I'll stay at some other Christmas village. I'm sure Lapland isn't short of them."

"There is one not too far."

"Great, I'll head over there then," I say, shrugging on my coat.

His jaw sets hard and he squares his shoulders. Damn, he's one big slice of Finnish pie. "Fine. You may stay."

"Great. Then I'm going to need a room."

"Fine," he grumbles again, picking up a key with a large candy cane hanging off it from the wall behind him. "I have one usable room left, but you're not going to like it."

CHAPTER FOUR

We walk to the back of the building where the path runs out, and I stand there with my suitcase wondering at what point the lumberjack receptionist is going to help me. Then he hands me a piece of rope. Attached to the end is a sleigh on which he places my suitcase.

My suitcase has its own teeny, little sleigh! OK. This is cute.

I think back to his last comment and all the keys hanging on the wall. Maybe I was wrong about the place being empty and they're all spares.

"You can't be doing that badly, if you're at full capacity," I say, as we trudge through the snow toward a row of wooden cabins. All around us are tall trees from every angle, each one drooping from the amount of snow on its boughs. It's weird to see so many trees but not hear birdsong. The silence is quite deafening.

"We're at ten percent capacity," he replies. "We used to offer thirty cabins, that's up to one-hundred-and-fifty guests as some are large family chalets, and now we only have three cabins full. Including yours."

I do some quick cabin math. Wow, OK, so he only has two families staying here.

"But, if you still have twenty-seven cabins left then why don't you have any rooms available?"

"We don't have any *working* rooms."

He stops walking for a moment, assessing me, as if wondering just how much he can tell me. Eventually, he lets out a long sigh. "There's something wrong with all of the cabins. Broken pipes, leaking roofs, cracked beams. They are not safe for guests."

I look around us at the empty cabins we're passing which are a mix of old and new styles, and all made of logs. Some are small and square, with triangular roofs and little chimneys — like a child's painting of a house. Others are larger and cylindrical in shape, with pointed roofs glittering white, like meringue peaks. They must be for bigger families.

I imagine they all once had foliage and tiny lights climbing up their porches and decorating their windows, maybe even wooden benches and their own Christmas trees. But these cabins are all dark and barren now. All except for one that glows orange and inviting in the distance. My chest flutters as I anticipate how cute my accommodation is going to look inside.

"Twenty-seven faulty cabins is a lot," I say. "Have you tried fixing them?"

He whips around like I've insulted his entire family. "Of course, I've tried fixing them. Do you think I'm stupid?"

I don't answer that. He keeps marching forward and I follow behind, my suitcase wobbling atop the teeny sleigh I'm dragging behind me. I feel like a child taking its teddy sled riding.

"And then what?" I ask. "What happens once you fix them?"

"And then everything in the cabins breaks again."

So no matter how often he fixes the rooms, everything keeps breaking? Maybe it *is* a curse. I will have to look into whether there are any Witches in Lapland.

"My cabin looks really cute and cozy," I say, as we approach the big glowing one with the twinkly lights.

"That's where I live," he replies.

Right. Of course, it is.

We keep walking in silence, the air biting at my cheeks and nose, nothing for miles around but snow-heavy trees and dilapidated cabins. Exactly how far away is my bedroom from reception and the only working part of this resort? I remember the map at the front of the village showing a candy store, a market, and an ice rink but all I see are empty cabins and snow upon snow.

Something catches my eye, something moving in the distance.

"Look!" I squeal, jumping up and down.

He stops. "That's a reindeer," Captain Obvious confirms. "There are too many around these parts. Only the tourists get excited about them."

"I *am* a tourist."

"You said you were a professional."

"I *am* a professional. A professional tourist."

He sighs heavily, a puff of hot air forming a cloud around him like a disgruntled dragon but doesn't say another word. He marches forward and I try to keep up, glancing over my shoulder as the reindeer disappears into the trees. I guess I'll take my Instagram-worthy photos later.

After trudging through the snow in silence for a few more minutes we finally arrive at a squat little cabin on the fringe of the ancient Santa town. It looks like a box made of matchsticks, with rotting logs jutting out of each corner. One wall has a door, the other three have windows that are badly in need of curtains and a good clean. If this decrepit cabin is the only *good* one left, I'd hate to see the inside of the others.

My guide's shoulders are so wide he can barely fit through the door as he maneuvers my suitcase into the room, leaving a wet puddle in his wake. I look around and shudder, although this time it has nothing to do with the cold.

Everything inside is wooden, from the floor to the walls, to the beamed vaulted ceiling. There's a sagging single bed in the corner, covered in a ratty patchwork quilt that looks like it was hand-stitched the day the village opened two centuries ago. A fireplace stands cold and empty on one side, and tea-making facilities on the other. What could have been a cute reading corner, complete with an armchair and bookshelf, looks more like two pieces of furniture left out for the trash. It's not so much that everything is old, but that everything looks like it's been tampered with. Destroyed. How did it get this way?

Maybe it will look nicer in the light.

I run my hand blindly along the wall until I hit a switch and flick it. A flash of bright sparks jolt through me and I jerk back hard, dropping to the floor with a squeal.

"Ow ow ow!!!" I shake my hand out trying to relieve the fiery pain.

The man stares down at me crouched on the ground. "You've been electrocuted."

"I fucking know that, Mister Health And Safety."

"Don't be dramatic," he bends down. "It happens sometimes."

"I don't know how many Club Meds you've visited," I shout at him as I get back up. "But getting electrocuted is not a standard hotel experience."

He pulls an exposed wire out of the wall and scowls at it.

"I keep fixing the electrics and they just break again the next day. I don't understand. Anyway, you will be fine."

He turns to leave, and I reach out and grab his arm. It's as hard as a tree branch.

"You can't leave me like this. Where's my warm welcome? The glühwein? A roaring fire? Clean towels? Food!"

He looks at me, perplexed. The Finnish are really good at staring.

"Dinner is ready, but there's no blood dumpling soup left," he says.

I make a face. "I think I'll survive."

"You can have the reindeer stew instead."

I think of the cute fluffy deer I saw earlier. My stomach has been grumbling since the airport but I'm not in the mood for a side-serving of guilt with my main course.

"Reindeer stew? I can't eat that!"

"It's what we eat here," he says. "It's our custom."

"But reindeer are so sweet. We just saw one. How could you eat that cute animal?"

His eyes narrow again.

"Are you one of those vegans?" he growls.

"No."

"Cows are cute. Pigs are cute. Sheep are cute."

"Yeah, yeah, I get the picture. Reindeer stew it is, I guess." He turns to leave. "Wait! Can you at least tell me your name?"

"Elias."

I think back to Jackson's briefing. "I thought the owner here is called Ilkka?"

A somber expression passes over Elias' face.

"Ilkka is my father. He's on a work trip right now."

Ping. Why lie about that? What else is this man hiding?

We both stand there in silence, then he looks at his watch.

"You've missed dinner now," he says. "It's served at six, which was seven minutes ago."

"What? No alternative dinner menu in the room? No wine list and cocktail of the week?" I call out to his retreating back.

"We don't do room service!" Elias snaps, slamming the front door behind him. The walls shake, and a lump of snow falls *inside* of the room.

"Can't wait to work with you!" I call out after him.

CHAPTER FIVE

Twenty minutes later there's a knock at my door and I find a steaming bowl of stew on my doorstep. It seems Elias reconsidered and brought me room service, but took off before I could thank him. Good, I'm glad that model-looking lumberjack didn't have time for small talk, I don't want to hear him Abercrombie and Bitch any more than I have to.

I pick up the bowl and breathe in the rich gravy, my stomach letting out a low rumble. I hate to admit it, but it smells amazing. The shredded meat is soaking into the creamiest mashed potatoes I've ever seen, and it's even garnished with crushed lingonberries and parsley. Fancy.

I take my meal to the couch, singing *All I Want for Christmas is...Reindeer STEW.* With each bite an eruption of flavors comes to the surface; ale, onions, bacon, rich gamey meat, and I continue humming my song through a full mouth of food to distract myself from the animal I'm chewing on. I think back to Elias and the pastry on his nails and flour on his apron. OK, so the miserable man can cook.

While I eat I manage to navigate the shitty WiFi and log on to the Blood Web to message Jackson.

Hi Boss, I've survived my flight to Finland and am currently in the heart of Lapland. The owner is more Christmas sneer than Christmas cheer and I'm already freezing my tits off. Hope you're happy.

Jackson's reply is swift. Poor guy spends his life living on the Blood Web.

I'm happy to hear you survived your SHORT flight. I'm sorry to hear about the state of your tits, though I think it would be very un-bossly of me to wish them a speedy recovery. Now stop messing about and please get back to work.

I smile, despite myself. Jackson's too serious for his own good but he can still banter till the Shifter cows come home.

The stew has filled me up and warmed me up, which means I should get out of these damp, coffee-stained clothes, wrap up in as many layers as I can, and start investigating.

I inspect the light switch, peering closely at the wires. They look like they've been bitten through. Rats? Yet Elias said everything at the resort keeps breaking — rats don't affect plumbing or cause wood rot.

If all this is really a curse, I'm going to have to question him about his family history and discover why anyone would want to haunt or hex him. Aside from the fact he has a terrible personality.

I run my finger along a dusty doorway, holding the dirt

up to the light, pretending I'm a character on *Supernatural* and the dust mites might be haunting clues.

I return to my laptop and log in to the Blood Web again.

Jackson, I'm considering that the village may be messed up because of a haunting. Or a Witches' curse. OR, hear me out, the village could be positioned over some ancient reindeer burial ground!

I eat the rest of the (actually really tasty) stew as I await his response. My screen lights up.

*Well done on all your hypothesizing, Saskia. Wouldn't it be great if we could send someone there to investigate and **actually find out the answer**? Oh to live in a world where that was possible.*

Rolling my eyes at his sarcasm, I decide cleanliness is more important than good-at-my-job-ness and go run a bath — but all that comes out is a dribble of icy cold brown water accompanied by a loud clunking sound. The walls are shaking. I quickly turn off the faucet and go to the sink instead.

There's no warm water there either. I may as well be bathing in a glacier, but at least this time it's running clear and quiet.

Shivering on the cold wooden floor before an unnecessarily large window I splash under my arms and between my legs, the whole while shaking like a leaf and telling myself I'll be warm in a minute.

Something catches my eye and I duck down as if that will protect my modesty, laughing out loud when I realize what it is. I stand up again. It's just another reindeer out in the snow, staring at me.

"Hey, cutie pie," I coo, tapping on the glass. I doubt he can hear me, let alone understand, but he looks so beautiful framed in the window with snowflakes falling on his fluffy snout.

With a snort, he shakes his head and runs off.

I rub myself dry with a greying towel that's as soft as sandpaper, wrap it around me, and run into the bedroom. I'm still shaking as I rifle through my suitcase, pulling out thermal underwear, two sweaters, thick leggings, and two pairs of wool socks. I laugh as I hold up the short red dress and heels I also packed. What exactly did I think I'd be doing? Stripping under the mistletoe?

Buttoning my coat up to my throat and wrapping my scarf around me tighter, I step outside to take a good look around.

Despite its initial decrepitness, I can see how this village was once kind of adorable. Veering past a few dark cabins, some of them with cracked windows and broken wooden railings, I walk past what was once Mrs. Claus' candy shop and peer into the window. It looks like no one has been inside all year, which is a shame because it's really pretty inside. Rows of bulbous glass jars full of glittering candies line the countertop and shelves, and there's an old-fashioned gold register at the center. I note the cobwebs connecting the glass jars and the layer of dust on the counter and wonder why such a cute little store is just sitting there, rotting away, right amid the Christmas season.

I follow the signs to reception, passing old streetlamps dotted around the ground like something from Narnia. Most of them are unlit, yet I half expect Mr. Tumnus to jump out at me.

As I round the corner I gasp. Jutting up to the star-filled

sky is a huge decorated Christmas tree. Fresh snow lays thick and plump on the branches, like peaked mounds of cream, weighing down each bough and the fading glow of twinkling lights beneath. Giant baubles peak through the snowy foliage — emerald green leafed in gold, swirls of burgundy, silver, and glittering purple, and star-like gilded tree ornaments that look like sparklers.

As I step forward something crunches underfoot. Colorful shards have turned the snow into a stained-glass mosaic thanks to a pile of smashed baubles. The damage looks like it's recent as the glass isn't buried by snow. Why are tourists so inconsiderate?

Surrounding the tree are more little cabins, the main building, a strange triangular-looking wooden tepee hut that may be an outside toilet, and what looks like a storage shed. I couldn't find much information online about what this resort offers but judging by another hand-painted sign stuck to the side of one of the cabins you can visit Santa's grotto, enjoy sleigh rides, and take part in cooking classes.

They say the snow muffles sound, but for a so-called village, this place is deathly-silent. I strain to hear something, anything, and I pick up the faint rumble of cars on the main road and the howl of a wolf. Oh god, not wolves. What if there are Werewolves nearby?

Wait, no. That's the howl of dogs. Huskies! OK, now I'm excited. Maybe I can find some clues amongst the huskie kennels.

I trudge through the snow, following the excited yelps of the dogs, until I finally find a ramshackle hut surrounded by a wire pen. It's full of gray and white dogs that bound up at the fence, licking and pawing at me. There are even a couple of puppies! All thoughts of Paranormal investigations are forgotten as I check there's no one around (of course, there isn't) then let myself into the unlocked enclosure.

At least a dozen dogs jump up at me, tongues lolling out of their mouths, their cold paws pushing me to the ground where they lick my face and pant puffs of hot air into clouds around me.

In the corner of the enclosure are a row of wooden sleds and lots of leather reins hanging up. At least this part of the village remains undamaged.

"What's been going on around here, eh?" I ask them.

But these aren't Werewolves or Shifters, they're just regular fluffy puppies and doggies with no answers to any mysteries.

I rub my face into their soft fur and pet them until I decide I'm too tired to ask any humans any questions and I return to my freezing cold cabin.

It's stupid to think I can do anything without a good night's sleep. Let's hope the bed and the blankets are at least in good working order.

CHAPTER SIX

I slept in all my clothes last night, and I was still cold. I found an old hot water bottle, but with only icy water to work with and no electricity that was of no use to me either.

According to my phone, it's nearly eight o'clock in the morning. Urgh, it still feels like midnight. The days are just as dark as the nights here, so I guess I may as well get up and look around the village some more before I head to breakfast.

Layering myself up with scarves and thick gloves I head outside and blink at the stark white landscape against the black of the sky. How the hell am I meant to investigate anything when there's no daylight?

I head in the direction of the main building, squinting through the gloom and trying the doors of each dark cabin I pass along the way.

Most of them are unlocked and once inside it's easy to see why most of them are uninhabitable.

In one hut I find shredded electrical cords, smashed windows, and one of the beds has even had the stuffing pulled out of the mattress. Who would do that? Do reindeer break into cabins and chew on furnishings and cables? Could those sweet excitable Huskies do this? I don't think so.

I enter another cabin and find all the cups in the cupboards smashed, the toilet bowl cracked, and the faucets stuffed with moldy leaves.

I find similar things in five more cabins; everything from holes in the roof and blocked chimneys, to broken tables and crumbling walls.

This looks like a mix of human vandalism and lack of maintenance, not anything magical. I don't know many Paranormals whose main choice of evil is causing household repairs. Elias just needs to invest some time and money into this place and give it some TLC.

I head to the main road wondering what the locals have to say about all this. I should probably speak to someone, and ask some questions, but I haven't seen anyone since I arrived.

The sound of an engine revving behind me makes me jump and I step aside as a bright red, King Ranch Ford pickup truck speeds by, showering me in slushy grey snow.

My legs are soaked. Does anyone ever stay dry around here?

I go full New Yorker. "I'm walking here, ya jerk!" I shout out to the dimming tail lights. Then the car stops and starts reversing.

Oh, shit!

The car comes to a halt beside me, and as the window slowly winds down the scent of fake strawberry hits me, followed by a cloud of vape steam.

"Need a lift?" a guy in a suit and Stetson says in a Texan accent. The inside of his car is cream and…is that an ostrich interior? Who the fuck has ostrich leather seats? "Are you lost, little lady?"

It's weird to see anyone in a pinstripe suit in the middle of the Nordic wilderness, let alone this cowboy.

"I'm fine. I'm staying here," I reply, signaling to the cabins, which clearly look empty and unused.

"Why would you spend your vacation here?" he sneers. He reaches into his pocket and hands me a card. "You want to find yourself a little bit of luxury, missy."

I read the business card out loud.

Mr. Michael Walker
Christmas World, CEO
The largest Christmas village in Lapland!

He taps the card in my hand with the tip of his vape.

"We have four hotels to choose from, heated inside and outdoor water parks, and the world's first virtual reality grotto. It's nothing like this..." he gestures at the village behind me. " ...trash."

This guy is like the Christmas village version of an Avon rep and I suddenly feel very defensive, like I did in the airport yesterday. So what if The Crazy Reindeer is a mess and the owner's a dick — at least Elias is trying. I think.

"Well, I like it here."

"Suit yourself."

Without so much as a goodbye the man speeds off in the direction of the car park, spraying me with yet more sludge, and I continue my fruitless task of investigating outside. I'm not exactly sure what I'm looking for, but other than the odd loose paving slab and a cracked window, nothing appears too out of the ordinary.

I'm nearly at the main building when I notice a string of

40

twinkly lights hanging down outside one of the nearby cabins. Maybe it came loose, or the wind blew it down, but either way it's not hard to re-hang some lights. Elias needs to get his act together.

I balance on the railing and hook the lights back up, switching them on at the wall and grinning as the porch sparkles like a Christmas tree. Cute. See? That wasn't so hard.

I jump back down and turn around to survey my handiwork, only to find the lights not only back on the ground, but each tiny bulb crushed and dead.

What the...?

OK, maybe there's more to this than I thought. A shiver runs through me, and I realize that on top of being extremely creeped out I'm also beginning to feel hungry. I forgot to ask what time breakfast is served.

With a groan I follow the signs to the main building, my feet already aching from the long trudge. In the distance I spot the suited guy walking around the complex, looking inside the darkened windows of a nearby cabin. What the hell is he doing? I guess the same thing I was — being nosey.

My stomach rumbles again so I keep going, my hunger mounting as I approach the main building, and the scent of baking fills the air.

Stepping inside, the warmth of reception surrounds me like a thick comforter, and I stop for a moment to let my bones thaw. I didn't note where the restaurant was, but the aroma of freshly made bread and something with cinnamon assaults my senses causing my stomach to let out another huge growl. There are no signs pointing to a restaurant, so I follow my nose instead, finding myself back in reception.

It's empty — surprise, surprise — but I can hear the clatter of utensils and the soft hum of people talking. I peer around the corner. Finally! The dining hall.

It's a lot larger than I expected, with a high beamed ceiling and walls adorned with antlers and deer heads. Last night's stew churns in my stomach. Poor Rudolph. A large stone fire is roaring at the back of the room, with piles of logs neatly stacked beside it, and woolen stockings hanging off the mantel. A large table in the center of the room has been laid out like it's Christmas day, with bright red cloth napkins and chipped wine glasses.

The table is empty save for a quiet, sullen family of four at the far end. That's it, the full extent of guests this morning. One of the small children starts crying and the father whispers something about seeing Santa later. The kid's eyes widen with excitement and I smile at him. This would have been my dream vacation as a child. OK, maybe not this exact place with its creepy dead animal heads staring down at me…but a fancier version.

I look around for a waiter, then notice breakfast is a buffet. How many people has Elias cooked for, considering it looks like there are only five of us left in this place now?

Upon a red checked cloth are flour-dusted wheels of barley bread suspended on a stand made of birch, and besides that a cast iron pan of scrambled eggs, stacks of pancakes, waffles, and pastries, and a collection of cute little jars which look like artisanal honey and home-made jam. I read the labels — lingonberry, cloudberry, elderberry. Who knew there were so many berries?

There's also a platter of smoked fish next to some mysterious cold cuts, which I'm hoping aren't reindeer. Those animals need to keep away from this joint!

I pick up a pastry that has a sign beside it which reads 'Karelian pies' and take a bite. I was expecting the inside to be apple or meat, instead, it's rice pudding. Damn, this stuff is good! I finish it all, the rice pudding oozing out over my hands.

OK, so this is not Christmas at The Ritz, but at least the owners of this place get full marks for authenticity. I can't believe Elias made all of this, but he must have because I don't see any other staff. Good to see the haunting, curse, whatever-it-is hasn't managed to get its hands on the food yet.

Talking of hands, I need to wash mine because they're now sticky with sugary rice pudding. The restroom is back in reception, so I turn back. But as I exit the bathroom, wiping my wet hands on my sweater, I hear an irritated voice coming from Elias's back office.

I'd recognize that booming, self-entitled voice anywhere!

It's Mr. Walker, the Texan vaper jerk who gave me his business card, and it sounds like he's arguing with the inn owner about something. I duck behind a wooden pillar wrapped in tinsel and peer through the open office door.

"You refused to answer my calls, so I decided to come and see you in person," Walker says.

"Can't talk right now," Elias replies in English, his voice sounding strained as if he's holding back a lot of rage. "Way too busy."

Walker isn't listening. "This won't take long. As I explained in the documents I sent you, we are interested in the purchase of The Crazy Reindeer…"

"No."

"You know," says Walker, "you could still manage the place, and we could get you some much-needed staff…"

"We're doing just fine," Elias snaps.

Ping. Poor Elias.

I flatten myself against the pillar as the inn owner storms off, Walker close behind him. Luckily the reception area has remained empty and the room echoes, so I can still hear every word they say.

"We would keep the resort exactly as it is," the businessman states. *Ping*. I jump at the unexpected lie. "We have no intention of destroying Finland's oldest Santa village."

Another *ping*. Why is this guy so eager to buy the place if he plans to change it?

"My family business, my family *home*, is not for sale," Elias growls.

"From my understanding, it's not much of a family business anymore. It's just you, and this place is far too much for one person to run. It's falling apart, Elias. I have offered you above and beyond what this resort is worth. Let me help you."

He's telling the truth. But that doesn't make sense. If he knows the place is worthless, and he plans to knock it down, why choose this place? What's so special about Elias' land? All I've seen is a clump of trees, a craggy hill, a small road, and a load of decrepit wooden buildings.

Walker gives Elias a business card and holds out his hand to shake. Elias refuses it, shaking his head instead, and turns his back on the businessman.

"I don't know how many times I have to tell you; this place is not for sale. Build another of your glitzy Santa Villages elsewhere," he says over his shoulder as he walks away, ripping up the business card into tiny papery snowflakes. "Your American tourists don't want the real Finland, anyway. They want hotdogs and hot Elves. You can keep that shit. We're happy as we are!"

Elias is telling the truth. He's never going to sell to this man. But with the last line, I hear the tell-tale *ping* and my heart sinks. He's not happy and he's not doing fine. Well, of course, he isn't. No one with his bad attitude is having a good time.

The Texan crosses the reception and leaves the building in a cloud of strawberry-scented vape. I look at the card Walker gave me earlier and type in Christmas World on my phone. WiFi is better in reception and straight away his website pops up.

Oh my god, he wasn't lying about owning the finest Santa Village chain in the world!

I scroll through the pages, each one getting more and more elaborate. There's a 24/7 cinema that only shows Christmas movies, six restaurants, an ice rink with a giant ice sculpture in its center, and themed bedrooms. I look around at the lobby I'm standing in then back to the website, and my heart sinks. Elias should give up. There's no way he'll ever be able to compete with Walker's 'Disney on ice' spectacular.

Still focusing on my phone, I go down the stone steps to the restaurant, eager to try some of those amazing berry jams and another Karelian pastry.

I haven't quite cracked this grand everything-keeps-breaking investigation yet, but so far I *have* learned that the oldest and most rundown Santa village in all of Finland, with the rudest owner who is mysteriously covering for his absent dad, doesn't want to sell the resort to a very rich and eager Texan. There's no investigation here. I can't help it if Elias is both rude *and* stupid.

I look up from my phone. Wait. Where the hell has the restaurant gone? And my pastries?

The long dining hall table has gone and in its place is a large wooden throne on a platform, surrounded by wrapped gifts, and a reindeer.

A real reindeer!

What the fuck is a reindeer doing in the dining room? I look around me, half expecting Elias to come running out of the kitchen brandishing a large knife and screaming, *"Anyone for reindeer carpaccio?"*

"Are you in the line?" a woman asks me.

She's holding the hand of a little ginger girl no older than three or four. The girl's cheeks are pink like she's been playing in the snow, and she's clutching a drawing she's done in crayon.

Behind them, a line has formed of parents and children all staring wide-eyed at the reindeer and the empty throne. Where did all these families come from?

I crouch down beside the child. "What's this?" I ask in Finnish, looking at a load of scribbles.

"A list for Santa," she says with a lisp. "He's on his way."

Right. Santa's appearance.

Oh well, I may as well stay for that. Maybe I can ask him for a decent fucking meal and a room with hot water for Christmas.

Festive music starts to play and a soft jingle of bells sounds from the speakers on the wall. The kids swivel their heads back and forth excitedly. The reindeer, which is definitely real and not tied to anything, stays perfectly still as a door opens and a man in a red suit walks in.

The room descends into a hushed silence. Santa is tall, broad, and walking like he has a meeting to get to. He doesn't even look at the children but heads straight to the throne and sits down with a huff. It's Elias.

He notices me at the front of the line and scowls, making his stupid Santa hat slip off his head, and I howl with laughter.

This place is too much. I'm laughing so hard I nearly vomit up my rice pudding pastry.

CHAPTER SEVEN

An hour has passed and I'm still waiting patiently on the sidelines of the dais for Elias to finish playing Santa. I'm in two minds about whether to stay, go back to New York, or spend Christmas in five-star luxury over at Christmas World. I don't particularly want to support that Texan jerk, but maybe *all* Christmas village owners are idiots.

Although Elias isn't doing too badly himself today. For such an empty village, there are a lot of kids here.

I was also surprised to see a Mrs. Claus turn up shortly after Elias began his shift. She's a stout elderly woman with rosy cheeks and a mulled wine smile, but I haven't had the chance to speak to her yet.

Elias greets child after child, listening to their lists with the face of someone who would prefer to be out in the woods alone than surrounded by excitable pre-schoolers, then gestures to each one to move on to Mrs. Claus who dutifully gives them a small parcel of cookies.

I didn't notice him at first, but there's also a guy dressed as an Elf snapping photos of the children. He's swaying far too much to be sober and his outfit looks like it's been made from different pieces of old green sheets sewn together.

I'm not laughing anymore. It's all kind of sad actually, like a middle school production of the Nutcracker; the papier mache and fingerpaint edition.

Mrs. Claus has the face of a woman who has seen a lot of Christmases, with each one getting progressively worse.

What a weird trio — grumpy young Santa, tired old Mrs. Claus, and a drunken Elf.

At least the kids seem happy. They all appear to be mostly locals, I soon realize, picking up on the Finnish. Makes sense. I don't imagine tourists going for this much Hullu Poro authenticity. I Googled The Crazy Reindeer and, although a few years ago all the reviews and blogs about this place were glowing, raving about how quintessentially Finnish it all was, the recent articles are full of exposés about guest accidents, broken amenities, and chronic understaffing.

So why are so many locals still coming here if its demise has made it into the newspapers?

Clearing my throat I approach the nearest mom in the line.

"Hi, there!" I smile at the five-year-old hiding behind her leg. "I'm a tourist exploring Lapland and I was wondering if this is the best Christmas village around or if there are any others you could recommend?"

"Best?" the woman laughs, but not in a mean way. "No, Hullu Poro isn't the *best* — far from it — but it's the one we keep choosing."

"I want to go to Christmas World," the little girl exclaims, before hiding in her mom's skirt again.

"Bah," the mother tuts. "Christmas World is cheesy. Not authentic." She looks around the room. "Yes, it's a lot fancier but… we just prefer Hullu Poro."

"What do you like about it?"

I look around, desperately trying to find one thing that would make it more appealing than...literally anywhere else. The girl runs off and the mother watches her, her eyes drifting over to Elias sitting on his throne, piercing blue eyes shining beneath his floppy Santa hat and arms too thick for his costume.

Oh. *Right*! Elias is the main attraction. The resident SILF — Santa I'd Like to Fuck. Literally, the only thing around here drawing the crowds of bored moms.

"Hullu Poro is also the only Santa Village to give kids a free show," she adds. "For many of us, this is all we can afford. Unlike all other tourist destinations in Lapland, Elias and his family refuse to charge for meeting Father Christmas."

Hmmm, OK, so they come for the eye candy *and* the generosity. I look at Elias in his Santa outfit again and my tummy does a little flip. I get it, I see the attraction; even if his chiseled, stubbly jaw, and messy blonde hair, are all hidden beneath a fake bushy beard and hat. Although... I tip my head to one side. That crushed velvet suit and floppy hat combo sure are giving off some hot Santasy vibes.

Fine. I can see why these women might want to sit on Elias' lap, but I still wouldn't have pegged him for the charitable type.

"How long have you been coming here?" I ask the mom beside me.

"Forever. Visiting Santa at Hullu Poro is a tradition that has been passed down my family line for generations."

It's her child's turn to tell Santa what she wants for Christmas and the mother gives me a parting smile and steps up to the podium.

I stand back and watch the rest of the excitable moms and their equally excitable offspring approach Elias, exchange pleasantries, and beam with pride as their child hands him a list or a drawing. Mrs. Claus looks exhausted and at one point she sways like she's going to topple over, Elias' hand shooting out to steady her.

The reindeer stays still the entire time, posing with the children and Santa, while the Elf does his best to hide the bottle of vodka he has hidden in one of the stockings hanging on the mantel behind him.

I listen for *pings* and watch out for any strange cursed things happening — but everything is normal and mundane and exactly like every other Santa mall visit…just the budget version that smells of damp deer.

Finally, the last kid leaves and Elias stretches and groans, pulling down his false beard like a surgeon after a tough operation. He's aged ten years in the few hours he's been sitting on that large wooden chair. He looks as exhausted as the old lady and the drunk Elf. I'm almost not in the mood to tease him. *Almost.*

I point at the mismatched patches on his red suit. "Interesting Santa outfit."

"Costume room caught on fire two weeks ago," he says gruffly. "We had to improvise." He rubs his temple as if he's tired just thinking about it.

God, this place really has gone to hell and back. OK, maybe there *is* something Paranormal going on here. No one can have *this* much bad luck. Although I'm not familiar with any pyrotechnic Paras — ghosts definitely don't set clothes on fire.

Poor-man's-Elf is now blatantly doing shots of Koskenkorva by the bar and singing what appears to be a song about reindeer stew. The giant white reindeer in the corner looks at him sideways and huffs then trots out as if it can understand his song.

I consider talking to Mrs. Claus, but she's already gathering her things together. She shoots me a small smile and strokes Elias's arm in parting.

"I'll see you later, my love," she calls as she slowly makes her way to the door.

I watch her go then wiggle my brows at Elias.

"Looks like you and Mrs. Claus have a lot of chemistry."

"That's my mother."

Oh. "Well, she seems nice."

Elias grabs a broom and starts cleaning up the wrapping paper and cookie crumbs off the floor. "Aren't all mothers nice?" he asks.

I snort. "Not by a longshot. No."

He gives me a curious look, but I don't elaborate. He's clearly hating every second of working here, yet as he sweeps he's giving it his full attention. He's so focussed it makes me wonder if that's what he's like when he's cooking, and if he takes that much care over every detail in his private life too. If he even has one.

"What do you want?" he barks. I didn't realize I was staring.

"If you want my help figuring out why your village is falling apart, I'm going to need a tour of this place and the surrounding land. Plus, I need more details about what's been going wrong around here. There's a lot to investigate."

"Fine. Let's go."

"Now?" It's already late afternoon and I haven't even had lunch yet. "But it's dark."

"It's always dark."

"I'm really not in the mood to walk around for hours."

"We'll take the sleigh."

Sleigh?

CHAPTER EIGHT

I can't help but squeal as Elias leads me to a gated enclosure where we're greeted by half a dozen Huskies. They must recognize me from last time as they attack me with kisses as I sink to my knees to make it easier for all of them to reach. I don't even care that the snow is cold beneath my knees.

"PUPPIES," I squeal with delight, letting each dog take turns licking my face.

"These are fully grown," Elias says, with zero emotion in his voice.

I don't let on that I've petted every single one of his dogs last night, even the younger ones. I rub one of the white Huskies behind the ears. "But they're puppppiiiiiies to me," I coo in a silly voice.

"That's inaccurate."

"Who shat in your eggnog?"

"In my what?"

"Never mind." I get up, brushing snow from the snowsuit I insisted I change into, much to Elias' chagrin.

The dogs paw and whine at me as I watch Elias strapping some leather reins onto something. The sleigh!

Or, at least that's what it used to be. Although still small and made of light wood, the shape of it is full Miracle on 54th Street, with curved edges and a high back, except the red and gold paint looks like it's worn away, and in some places even scraped off.

I walk over to it and rub my fingertip along one of the scratches.

"Does that say...*Suck my baubles, Santafucker?*" I say, holding back a laugh.

Damn, the tourists around here aren't as sophisticated as I thought they would be. Graffiti is one thing, but defacing Santa's sleigh?

Elias huffs, his lips setting in a firm straight line.

"It appeared a few days ago." He shakes his head like he's more than done with this shit, and signals for me to get in the sleigh.

The inside is lined with furs and there's room enough for one person to sit in front with a big sack of presents between their legs, while I guess the driver stands at the back.

I stroke the soft grey fabric lining the seating area.

"Reindeer skin," Elias says, calling the dogs over.

Of course, it is.

Man, these six Huskies can *run*. I'm huddled in the seat of the wooden sleigh, a thick blanket thrown over my knees, and I'll admit I'm pretty cozy. Elias is towering behind me, a hand on either side of me as he manages the reins. It's strange to be sitting so close to someone yet facing away from them. If I were to turn around, I'd get a mouthful of his crotch. I keep very still, enjoying the strength of his arms and his commanding voice as he manages the dogs.

We glide over the snow at super speed as Elias points out different parts of his village. I count the cabins as we pass them. There are thirty in total.

"Three are in good working order," he says.

"Including mine?" Which most definitely *isn't* in good working order.

"Yes. And mine."

Right. So my calculations were correct this morning, he now has just *one* paying customer. That miserable-looking family I saw at breakfast must have thought they'd landed a great online deal until they saw where they were staying.

We head towards a cluster of birch and pine trees. Everywhere I look is bright and white, slashed with shadows of black and silver. A lantern swings above my head, creating a golden pool around us. Neither of us speaks and I soak up the silence, just the swoosh of the sleigh in the snow and the panting of the dogs sending clouds of breath-smoke into the air.

"What's that?" I ask, pointing at something in the distance. It looks like collection of tents or tables.

"It used to be a market," he says. "Local traders would come out here for the season, our customers loved it. But the locals have started saying the area is cursed, so it's been abandoned all year."

We pass more cabins that look like holiday homes, an empty café, and what appears to be a long-forgotten gift shop. It seems there was once a small village here, adjacent to the Santa village. Perhaps it was where all the workers lived.

"And all this is your land?" I ask.

Elias grunts, which I take as a 'yes'. So he's not only lost money at the Santa village but all these people's rent too.

The buildings are silhouetted sharply against the bright

snow, like dark ancient ruins. It's hard to imagine that just a year or two ago this was a bustling tourist attraction. Some of the buildings are beyond repair.

"What happened there?"

"Roof caved in."

"And there?" I point at the gift shop.

"Flooding."

"Are *any* of the buildings OK?"

"The workshop, which is where I'm taking you now."

Each time Elias speaks he has to bend down closer to me and I feel his breath against the exposed back of my neck. I shiver and sink deeper into the furs.

"What do you make at the workshop?" I ask.

"Toys, of course."

Of course, because Elias is a Hallmark movie in flannel — albeit a slightly decrepit and outdated one on VHS.

After fifteen minutes the Huskies bring us to a small cabin on the outskirts of the birchwood forest. He sure does have a lot of land to look after. I think back to Walker and his offer. It must have been a hefty sum of money, but I still don't get it. If the locals think the area is cursed, why would Mr. Pinstripe want to invest so much into it?

"This is our toy workshop," Elias announces as we pull up to a quaint little hut that looks like it's straight out of Hansel and Gretel. I smile to myself, imagining what Elias would say if I told him I was the Witch of the story.

"It looks old," I say.

"It is. This is where it all began. My great-grandfather was a toymaker, the only one in the village. He built our business from this very cabin."

Elias calls out a command and the dogs stop obediently, panting excitedly as he helps me out of the sleigh. It takes all my strength not to go over and play with them again.

The door of the cabin creaks as we step inside, Elias having to duck so as not to hit his head on the doorframe.

It looks more like a doll's house inside than any kind of Santa's Little Helpers workshop. The room is lit by a large fire in the corner and lots of candles, with wooden workbenches running along the center of the room. Upstairs there's a mezzanine level where I can hear a sewing machine, and several different stations are dotted around — one for gluing, one for painting, one for sanding.

"Everything we make is from local wood," Elias explains, nodding at the birch forest out of the window. "We still receive orders from a few nearby gift shops and local families."

His face is cast in shadows, still and focused, but I can see a kind of sadness in his eyes.

As my vision adjusts to the candlelight, I'm able to count the number of workers. Three. Just three people hunched over the wooden toys in their hands. How can anyone work in such dim light?

"I didn't know kids still play with wooden toys," I say, running my finger over a brightly-painted wooden horse.

"It's tradition."

Elias picks up a Santa figurine from the table and blows the dust from it. I wonder why this building was unaffected like the others.

The workers are all old. They look as if they've been sitting at their little tables since Elias' great-grandfather built the place.

"Do they make the toys?" I whisper, nodding at an old man sanding a little figure of an elephant.

"Yes. They have worked here for as long as I can remember. They are like family."

Elias introduces me to the elderly man, Matti, who's moved on to painting the toy elephant. Behind him Tapio, the carver, takes a break from whittling a firetruck and waves at me. Johanna, a kind-looking lady with a long plait of silver hair running down her back, is attaching strings to pull-along horses.

"Why are they working so late and in the dark?" I whisper to Elias. I don't know anything about Finnish trade laws, but surely these elderly workers shouldn't have to sit here making toys by candlelight?

"They choose their hours. We get very little daylight this time of year anyway, but with Christmas coming up and children counting on us, they insist on sleeping upstairs and working around the clock."

"How can they see what they're doing? Why don't they switch the light on?"

He rubs his face; the candlelight casting shadows over his tired features. "They used to make the toys in the newer workshop next to reception. The three of them would dress up — the kids loved watching Santa's Elves make their toys. But then the fuse box exploded last month so we've had to move them here."

"Was it a matter of Elf and Safety?" I ask.

He ignores me, still staring into the distance. "This was my great grandfather's toy workshop. It doesn't have any electricity, but they don't mind. It reminds them of the old days."

I stop cracking my un-punny jokes, my chest aching as I imagine Elias here as a little boy, watching the same three people make toys alongside his grandfather. This place must mean so much to him.

I wander around and nearly stumble into three giant pots of paint, but Elias reaches out for me before I make the world's biggest mess.

"Would you like some tea?" Johanna asks me, pointing to the small gas stove in the corner. The light of the fire picks out every one of her wrinkles, and when she smiles I see her dimples so deep it's as if they are carved out of wood.

"We have Christmas stars," the old lady says, holding out a tray of Joulutorttu, traditional Finnish tarts made with flaky pastry and prune jam. "I made them myself."

I think back to the rice pudding pastries I had this morning and take one, my stomach instantly letting out a low rumble I hope no one heard.

"These are incredible," I say, through a mouthful of soft cookie.

Elias takes one and smiles kindly at Johanna, a rare smile that lights up his whole face. He should do it more often. His smile widens further as I compliment her and grab two more.

The fireplace in the cabin takes up an entire wall and I'm suddenly very hot. I take off two layers, letting the tea I've just been given warm me up further, and take a seat beside the fire.

"Tell me what it used to be like here," I say to the workers as they join Elias and me. They seem happy to have company, fussing around me and plumping up cushions.

"As children, we were told to keep away from the woods, but we knew they were made of magic," Matti says, pointing outside the window at the dark shadows blowing in the bitter wind. The other two cackle with laughter.

"We would chase butterflies and say they were Fairies," Johanna adds. "We would scare one another with stories of trolls and ogres, and every time we heard something rustle in the undergrowth, we'd say the Pixies and Elves were coming to get us."

I know for a fact Elves hate going anywhere near children — but I don't tell her that.

"And Hullu Poro?" I venture. "When did that all change?"

They look at one another, mumble something about Elias

and his poor father, then go back to telling me what fun they had as children playing amongst the magical trees. Why don't they want to talk about all the bad luck over at the Santa village? Do they also think it's a curse? Or one of the magical beings they believed in as children?

"We don't have to stay here long," Elias says to me quietly, shifting uncomfortably in his seat. "They can get a bit nostalgic sometimes. Very few people visit them this time of year."

"No rush. I have all the time in the world," I tell him, placing my hand on his arm. He looks at it for a moment then lets out a long sigh, not out of irritation but as if he finally has permission to relax. Even if it's just for an hour or so.

"Tell me more about these legends," I say to Johanna. Her face lights up with excitement and she insists I eat more cookies as she paints a picture of snow-covered woods and icy lakes teeming with evil lurking in every shadow. I know all about monsters, but everything she talks about is myth and legend. No Vamps, no Werewolves, no Witches. And her idea of Fae is nothing like the real thing.

With each story I watch Elias' face get more and more tense, dark shadows passing over his wide jaw and Nordic cheekbones. It's obvious he thinks their talk of mythical goat-men and creepy creatures is a bunch of gibberish, but likewise something akin to nerves dances behind his crystal blue eyes.

"Stop, Johanna," Tapio says, waving his wrinkled hand up and down. "You are making the boy scared. It hasn't been easy for you this year, has it, Elias, my dear?"

Elias gives Tapio a kind smile and pats his hand. "I'm managing just fine. I'm not worried at all."

My eyes are drooping, a mix of jet lag, cookie coma, and cozy-overload, but I sit up with a start at the two loud *pings* of Elias' lies have generated. He's *not* managing well, and he *is* worried. His hand is inches from mine, and I think about giving it a reassuring squeeze, but just as quickly he jumps up brushing crumbs off his lap.

"We better get going," he announces. "It's getting late."

The workers all give one another nervous glances and agree, before wishing me well and scuttling back to their workstations. In less than ten seconds we've gone from chilled fireside ghost stories to hurriedly putting on our hats and coats.

What's the rush? Do the Huskies have a bedtime?

CHAPTER NINE

I'm back in the sleigh and more than wide awake now as the bitter wind whips through my hair and stings my cheeks.

"Getting back to Hullu Poro will be quicker if we cut through the forest!" Elias shouts over my head. "Seeing as you've now seen everything."

"I thought Johanna said the forest was dangerous," I shout back.

He scoffs. "Don't believe all they told you. Those three love a tall tale."

I look up and study his features, the white landscape reflected in his clear eyes. He was built for this terrain. His face is tinged pink and gold from the cold and the light of the lantern. He's still wearing his floppy Santa hat and flecks of snow are settling on his overgrown stubble. His face shifts from pure concentration to concern.

"Hold on tight," he shouts, his gloved fists tightening on the reins by my head.

That's not what you want to hear when you're racing through the snow at night, sitting inside a wooden sleigh.

"What's wrong?" I shout out.

He tips his chin in the direction of the path. The wind is blowing so hard it's impossible to see the route through the trees, and the snow has gone from a light flurry to thick snowflakes like balls of cotton.

"The blizzards have become unpredictable here lately."

How do blizzards become unpredictable? Aren't they always unpredictable?

My question is soon answered as the wind picks up further, causing the snow to rise from the ground and flutter through the air in front of us. In an instant, the snow thickens in the air so much that I can hardly make out the Huskies at the front. I can hear them though, and something has them panicked.

Their running has become more erratic, accompanied by little yelps of surprise. What the fuck is going on? Surely these dogs are used to snowstorms? We're going so fast now my eyes are stinging and watering and I have to bury myself deeper into the blanket, which is now soaking wet and no comfort.

Elias yells at the dogs to slow down but they don't, it's like they're trying to free themselves from their reins.

With a loud crack, we hit a bump in the road and suddenly I'm flying.

A pile of powdery snow cushions my fall, but still knocks the air out of me on impact. Can you break a bone falling in snow?

Something hurts. *Everything* hurts.

I lay still for a moment, scared to move. Slowly I raise my head and blink three times, but my vision is shrouded by the thick white flurry of snow. I roll back my shoulders and hesitantly get to my feet.

OK, so I can walk. That's good. But I can't see. Everything is white and blurry like it's just me in the middle of a blank page. I can't make out the trees, the sleigh, Elias. I can't even hear the dogs anymore.

"Elias," I cry out. My voice is muffled like I'm shouting into a thick downy pillow. "Elias!"

This is impossible. We're too far away to walk back to the village and I wouldn't know which way to go anyway. The tall, skinny birch trees offer zero protection from this wind and I've lost my mittens.

"Elias!" I shout again, as loudly as I can.

I'm stumbling around, holding out my hands and hoping I will feel the wood of the sleigh or the fur of the dogs at some point — but everything is eerily silent. Perhaps the sleigh went on without me and Elias didn't realize I'd fallen off. Maybe he won't notice I'm gone until he gets back to the village!

I trip over something and land face-first in the snow, my bare hands stinging as they sink into the ground. I look back and feel for a log or rock, but there's nothing there.

I push my hair back from my face and massage my ankle. Shit! I think it's sprained. Pain rings through my entire leg as I attempt to put weight on it.

Fucking fantastic.

Suddenly, a high-pitched giggle erupts beside me, and something furry whips across my face. I scream, batting at the space in front of me. Something hard collides against my stomach. Then my back. A branch whips me across the arm, then something sharp sinks into the flesh of my arm. I scream out in pain.

What the fuck is going on?

But there's no one there. Nothing there. I feel another blow to the face, falling to my knees and shouting out again as I try to crawl away.

But whatever the hell is attacking me is now following me too. A trail of giggles accompanies me every time I attempt to stand, knocking me back down until I give up trying to get away and curl up into a ball. I can feel blood trickling down my arm, the fabric of my coat wet and sticky, and my ankle throbbing with pain.

Am I getting beaten up by a hoard of Finnish ghost children?

I stay curled in a ball with my arms covering my face for what feels like forever, flinching at the high-pitched squeals and giggles surrounding me and the jabs and pinches that still hurt through my thick clothing. Maybe I should have researched 'forest creatures of Finland' before coming out here. Not that I can think of any critters that like ganging up on humans and yanking their hair.

Something big grabs on to my coat and starts pulling. I peek out and see the velvety muzzle of a reindeer. Seriously? Is this a fucking free-for-all? I thought reindeer were herbivores.

I kick out at it but it has gripped onto the sleeve of my injured arm with its teeth, dragging me through the snow. I lash out, kicking it with my good leg, my grunts of pain merging with the animal's own impatient huffs.

Well, let go then, you fucking shit!

It clamps down harder and keeps dragging me. The light gets darker and darker until I find myself deep in the woods.

I can still hear the squeals and giggles of whatever attacked me before fading into the distance, and now I have this beast to contend with. I scream as loudly as I can and punch out blindly, my hand colliding with a wet snout. The reindeer squeals and stumbles backward.

"That's right, Rudolph the broken-nosed reindeer!" I hiss through clenched teeth. "Fuck off!"

But the animal is determined and keeps tugging at me, ramming its head into my side as I face-plant into more snow.

I can't believe I'm about to be mauled by a blood-thirsty reindeer just before Christmas.

"SASKIA!"

My chest tightens at the sound of Elias' unmistakably rough voice. He's nearby!

I grapple, trying to stand, but my hands just sink even deeper through the thick snow.

"Elias!" My voice sounds weak as it rings against the trees. "Elias! I'm here!" I shout.

I look over at the reindeer, aware that it's finally let go of my arm. Except in its place is a young man with long disheveled pale blonde hair full of dry leaves and squashed berries. A *naked* young man. And he's looming over me, staring, silently.

Elias emerges from the white mist with a face like thunder. His hair is damp, his coat ruffled and both gloved fists clenched, one hand clutching a ripped piece of the leather rein. If he's surprised by the fact a naked man is standing next to me, he doesn't show it.

He rushes to my side, falls to his knees, and gently peels off my coat to look at my arm. I didn't realize the snow around me has turned red with my blood.

Elias makes a face I can't decipher — a mix of anger, concern, and frustration.

"You need an infirmary," he says, looking up at the naked man. "Shift, Fjorn, for God's sake! You're going to freeze."

Before I have a chance to ask what the hell is going on, the young guy beside me shifts back into the form of a giant white reindeer and gallops away. So the reindeer was a Shifter and he was...*helping* me?

I'm starting to feel faint.

"I'll go get the dogs," Elias says in his gruff voice.

"What the fuck!" I shout. "You didn't tell me you have a Shifter friend. You're human. I'm pretty sure you're human, right? I didn't even know you *knew* about Shifters. For fuck's sake, Elias!"

"Language," he replies, examining my bleeding arm.

"Or what? The fucking trees will be offended?" I pull my arm away from his gentle touch, then immediately cry out with pain. "What is it with your crazy forests out here? Something tripped me up, then punched me in the face, I was getting poked and jabbed and bitten and whatever it was, it was... invisible."

"You need the infirmary."

The snow has settled, the air once again clear, the blizzard having stopped as quickly as it began. As if I weigh nothing at all, Elias scoops me up and carries me back to the sleigh where the Huskies are all waiting.

I wrap my arms around his neck, mainly from fear of falling again and out of sheer relief, but Elias keeps his steely eyes fixed ahead.

A Shifter reindeer, a forest full of invisible, violent whatever-the-hell-they-weres, and my clothes are completely soaked. Again.

I'm really starting to dislike Finland.

CHAPTER TEN

"We need to get your injuries seen to," Elias shouts over the howling wind while tucking the blankets around me. He's either unaware or unbothered by the fact I'm getting blood all over them.

"We need to talk about the fact you're friends with a man who can change into a reindeer."

Elias grunts and adjusts the reins.

"So we're not having that discussion?" I ask.

"You're hurt. Let's go."

"I have a Band-aid back in my cabin."

He rolls his eyes and steps behind me, and before I have a chance to argue or grab on, we're racing through the snow again.

"Hey, isn't your village that way," I shout as we speed past an old, faded sign.

"I'm not taking you back to Hullu Poro," he says. "You need to have that arm examined. And even if it's less serious than we think, my medical supplies went missing a few weeks ago."

It took nearly an hour to get here from the local airport,

and that was by car on an actual road, so unless there's some magical hospital igloo I didn't spot on the way to his toy workshop, then where the hell is he taking me?

"Christmas World has an infirmary," Elias says, as if reading my mind.

Christmas World? His competitor and Lapland's answer to festive Disneyland?

I know Elias wouldn't do this unless he thought I was very injured. I try to hone in on the pain but all I feel is a weird itchy sting on my arms and legs.

Whatever bit me my body is reacting like crazy to it.

I spot Christmas World as soon as we round the corner. Like some kind of snowy Vegas, it looms iridescent and shiny in the distance, a cornucopia of all things wondrous and magical.

Golden gates interlaced with streams of holly and ivy open up for us automatically as we head up the snowy path, to the delight of small children who think the Huskies and grumpy Elias still in his Santa hat, are part of the attraction.

Unlike Elias' village, this place is *packed*. It's nearing nine o'clock at night, yet you'd think it was the middle of the day.

Everywhere I turn I see families beaming huge, happy smiles, as hand-in-hand with their rosy-cheeked children they wander around the make-believe village. Chubby fingers point up at the sign of an old-fashioned candy store that's still open, another shop with bulbous-shaped windows displaying wooden Nutcracker soldiers, and a wooden pen full of fluffy reindeer you can feed.

I think of the naked guy in the woods a short while ago and turn to question Elias about him, but I'm distracted again by a huge ice-skating rink at the end of the winding path. It's in the center of a square surrounded by not one but eight Christmas trees and a real, live choir singing *Silent Night*.

How the hell is Elias and his 1950s ramshackle village meant to compete with this?

"This place is…"

"Disgusting," he says, finishing my sentence. "Nothing about this place means Christmas."

What?!

"*Everything* about this place is Christmassy," I cry as I notice the other side of the street is a festive market, each stall strung up with colourful lights displaying hand painted signs that read 'Organic Waffles', 'Spiced Nuts' and 'Birch Carvings'. I struggle to get out of the sleigh and stumble into Elias as I get to my feet, ignoring the pain in my throbbing ankle.

I turn slowly in a full circle, taking a deep breath. "It even *smells* of Christmas. Cinnamon, gingerbread, pine trees, wood smoke, toffee, cloves. Wait a minute….Do you think they have glühwein?"

"Why not?" Elias grumbles. "Everything else here is undecidedly non-Finnish. Why not enjoy a German tradition to go with your Russian ballet statues and your greedy American capitalism?"

"Whoa," I say, holding my hands out like a 'stop' sign. "Christmas is Christmas, no one owns it. It's a time of joy, and laughter, and shoe shopping."

"Are you quoting a song?"

"You're being a Grinch," I say, poking his arm. Oh, hard biceps.

"Michael Walker is only interested in money. This is nothing like The Crazy Reindeer. Our village encompasses tradition, the *real* Finland, our customs and local legends. It's about family and being at one with nature. Not about…"

I've already hobbled off.

"A Christmas-tree-shaped shooter!" I declare, holding up a hand-painted shot glass. According to a sign above my head, every item on that market stall is hand-blown and hand-painted.

"What time do you close?" I ask the woman standing by the stall. She's wearing red and green Lederhosen and a colorful pointed hat like a jester. "The market closes at 1 am," she replies, handing me a free candy cane. "But we have shows and festivities all night long."

I raise my eyebrows, taking a minty bite of the candy.

"Good evening, Elias," she says.

I feel him stiffen beside me, and he clears his throat. "Annelli," he replies, nodding politely. "I didn't know you worked here."

"You know each other?" I ask, the candy cane sticking my teeth together as I attempt a smile. My arm itches and burns with pain and my ankle is so swollen it's pressing against my boot, but it's so cold my entire body has virtually gone numb. I notice the woman look at my bloody, torn sleeve and the fact I'm standing on just one leg, but she doesn't say anything.

"Annelli used to work with me," Elias says. "Many of the staff here did. Until…"

She gives him a sorry smile then turns to a customer beside her buying a decanter and matching wine glasses depicting a scene from The Snowman.

"Come," Elias says, hooking his arm around me so I can lean into him. "Let's get that wound dressed. Animal bites can be dangerous."

"I had my rabies shot a few months ago when a rat bit me in Central Park," I say. Well, it was actually a rat Shifter, but that's beside the point. I go to ask him about the reindeer Shifter again but he interrupts me.

"You can get worse things than rabies here," Elias says.

Worse things than rabies?

I don't bother replying, suddenly acutely aware that my arm is really fucking hurting.

Elias holds me up as we venture further into the resort, with me hobbling as fast as I can to keep up with him. Head down, his strides gaining speed, Elias refuses to soak in any of the Christmas magic. Damn, he really does hate it here.

Someone else says hello to him, a guy this time, standing at a jewelry stall. Every item, whether silver or gold, is studded with lilac gemstones. Elias nods and keeps walking, but I make him stop so I can have a closer look at the sparkly stones. I hold one of the necklaces up to the light.

"Local amethyst," the man says.

Elias looks awkward around this guy, probably another employee he's lost, but I'm enthralled by the pretty jewel in my hand.

"I thought amethyst is mined in Brazil?"

The man smiles. "It's quite a common stone, but few people know Lapland has its own mine. And it's rumored that there are many that remain undiscovered."

That's the kind of boring factoid Jackson would watch a documentary about. I make a mental note to tell him, then I make another mental note to buy myself a memento. Actually, maybe I'll buy one for Mikayla's birthday in February. It's her birthstone. I will have found her by then — I will. She needs to know I haven't given up hope.

"Are you OK?" Elias asks. "You look like you're in a lot of pain."

I sniff and nod and he guides me by my good arm. "Come on, let's go before they shut the infirmary."

He leads me past a mechanical display of polar bears and penguins singing a happy jiggly Christmas tune, a guy dressed as Jack Frost dancing amongst the animatronics.

"Literally nothing to do with Christmas," Elias mumbles. "The habitats of polar bears and penguins are on different sides of the world. Neither of which is Finland. Christmas should be authentic, local, artisanal…"

"Yeah, I get it, Elias. Jeez, you really put the anal in artis*anal*."

Elias frowns at my joke. I don't care about his mood or that my whole body is screaming in pain — I'm in paradise!

"Oh my god!" I exclaim, pointing at a giant gingerbread house facade. "What's in there?"

"That's one of the restaurants," he replies.

One of them? And I bet they serve more than just reindeer stew. My stomach grumbles. One pastry, three cookies and a mini candy cane don't count as three solid meals.

"And that?" I say, hoping the other building serves food too.

"That monstrosity of a cabin," he says, pointing at a low wooden hut with Christmas wreaths as porthole windows, and a huge glittering red bow wrapped around it made of a million red LED lights, "is the infirmary."

"There are *doctors* inside there?"

"Just the one. But she's very good."

CHAPTER ELEVEN

W e push the door open and are greeted by a woman holding a clipboard. She's wearing a strange outfit consisting of a white baby doll dress with matching feathery wings and a halo.

"Elias!" Surprise spreads across her pretty face as soon as she sees him. "Come in! Come in!"

"Kari," he mumbles, nodding grimly in her direction before turning to me. "Saskia, this is Dr. Kari. She's a great doctor. You're in good hands."

Dr. Kari blushes and looks down, tucking a perfectly curled strand of hair behind her ear. There's tension here, and not the kind Elias had with the nice lady at the glass stall. These two clearly know, or *knew*, one another *very* well.

"What's with the get-up?" I ask. It comes out more confrontational than I intended.

Dr. Kari gives a very un-doctory giggle. "What? This old thing? It helps distract the kids from their injuries."

I force a smile onto my face. Something about this woman irks me. Her saccharine nature wouldn't last a day in New York.

She puts down her clipboard. "A new Hullu Poro staff member, I see. So, Elias, what happened this time?"

This time?

"Saskia doesn't work with me," he says, looking embarrassed.

"Oh, no. Another *guest?*" Walking me over to an examining table, Dr. Kari gently pulls off my snow boots. I wince at the pain in my ankle, groaning loudly as she peels off my fluffy sock to reveal a large blue lump sticking out of my foot the size of a mini eggplant.

She doesn't seem too concerned though as she's still talking to Elias.

"I thought the village was closed," she says. "I heard all the guests had left."

I don't pick up any malice or scorn in her voice, just resignation. As if she doesn't understand why he keeps going.

"Close The Crazy Reindeer just before Christmas? *Ridiculous.* We would never do that! The village is doing just fine."

I feel the *ping* of Elias's last lie as he crosses the room and looks out of the window. Even though it's getting late there are so many lights outside it could be midday. He watches the snow fall, his strong frame silhouetted in the dim glow of the room. The infirmary is warm, wooden, and full of little plastic lights that look like candles. I can't believe a medical room is cozier than my so-called accommodation.

"Saskia is helping me with a project," Elias says.

Dr. Kari doesn't reply, instead signaling that I need to take the rest of my snowsuit off so she can take a full look at my leg injuries. I wriggle out of my padded suit while his back is turned, leaving me with just a shirt and underwear on, a fleecy blanket covering up my middle. The doctor is still focussed on my feet.

"Your ankle is swollen but not broken or sprained," she

says, slowly moving it from side to side. "It should be fine by tomorrow."

She binds it with a thick, stretchy bandage, then moves up my legs, dabbing antiseptic on the cuts. I wince.

"Oh. What's this?" she says, peering closer at the gashes.

Great. Just what you want a doctor to say as they're examining your body.

She switches on a light above our heads and touches my skin lightly, her brow furrowing.

"Reindeer bites," I explain.

She lets out a light laugh, not entirely unkind. "No. Something smaller than a reindeer. A ferret? A chihuahua, maybe?"

Now I'm being bitten by ghost chihuahuas? Fucking great.

I clutch the blanket close to my chest as I give Elias a 'we need to talk' look.

I'm not aware of any ghosts that inflict corporal punishment, or of any specific curses where you end up bitten by hyperactive ferrets or beaten to near death by a blizzard. There also aren't any Paranormals who can turn themselves invisible.

This is ridiculous. I'm going to have to do more Blood Web research tonight.

"Where exactly did this happen?" the doctor asks.

"In the forest."

Dr. Kari lets out a gasp that sounds like a delicate hiccup. "Oh no, Elias. You really shouldn't be in the woods at night!" Her voice is gentle, full of worry. "You know better than that."

Elias grunts and shrugs his shoulders as if brushing away her concern. "Oh, come on, Kari! Don't tell me you believe those superstitious stories too. Children's tales. There's nothing scary in the woods. "

Ping.

I can't tell if he's lying to her or himself. I know Elias is aware of Shifters, it's not every day your friend goes from being a helpful reindeer to a naked dude in the snowy forest. Surely at this point, he's put two and two together and realized his village is suffering from more than your average case of tourist wear and tear.

I have no idea what the hell is going around here — but I do know this mystery is fishier than a Merman's scrotum.

"Did this…animal…bite you anywhere else?" she asks.

I point to my arm which she's only just noticed is covered in blood.

"Oh my goodness. Take off your shirt, please." She turns around. "Elias, some privacy."

Elias looks like there couldn't possibly be anything more unpleasant than seeing me naked, and bolts out the door leaving an icy draft in his wake.

It's just the two of us now so I carefully peel off my shirt. I'm not particularly pleased to be stripping in front of this woman, but luckily I'm not into the Scandinavian Barbie look. I prefer my women shorter, darker, and a little more bitter.

"I don't think there will be any lasting damage," she says, examining the wounds on my arm and applying the same serum she did on my legs. "Could have been a lot worse if it had occurred at Hullu Poro."

"I'm guessing I'm not the first injury you've dealt with from Elias' village?" I say.

She shakes her head. "Believe me, I've seen my fair share of bizarre Hullu Poro accidents. I've even been on the receiving end of a few…back when I…" She pauses. "Worked there."

It's an interesting loaded pause. I'm willing to bet my non-wonky ankle that the glowing angelic doctor used to date Elias and it didn't end well.

"How did you get hurt?" I ask.

"I broke my arm when a wardrobe fell on me, that was the first time, and a few weeks later I tripped on a bucket and twisted my ankle. The third time I was concussed when a tree branch fell on my head." She lets out a light laugh, even though it's clear neither of us is finding this amusing. "By then Elias insisted I stop working there. Christmas World was looking for a doctor, and it was a local job and paid well, so..." She opens up her hands as if to demonstrate she had no choice, but it's clear the decision still doesn't sit comfortably with her.

"That must have been a stressful time," I say, seeing if maybe some empathy will get her to open up more. "Are you usually that clumsy?"

She gives another sad laugh. "Not really," she says, cleaning the final wound and fetching something from the countertop. "Hullu Poro is riddled with bad luck. I truly believe that."

This doctor believes in a lot of hocus pocus for a woman of science.

"So you haven't injured yourself since?"

"No. I've been telling Elias to sell that place for years..." Her voice dips lower, "...before someone gets seriously hurt. Or worse."

I don't know — broken bones and concussions sound serious enough to me.

"This is my special homemade balm." She holds a small glass jar up to the light full of pearlescent cream. "It speeds up the healing." She applies it to each cut, bite and graze and immediately I feel an odd tingling sensation spread through along my arms, legs, and stomach. The room fills with the scent of something sweet that I recognize, but can't quite place. She finishes off her treatment by sticking a big band-aid covered in pictures of snowflakes on the largest of the bites.

The balm must have some kind of numbing agent in it as I can hardly feel any pain now.

"Do you miss working at Hullu Poro?" I ask her, conscious I'm running out of interrogation time.

"No."

Ping. She's lying. Though whether she misses the Christmas village or the man who's currently standing grumpily outside the door, I'm not sure.

CHAPTER TWELVE

"You've been so helpful," I say to the doctor as she assists me with my snowsuit and boots. Thanks to the warmth of the room everything is dry and toasty. She's put my injured arm in a sling and told me to rest it, but at least it no longer stings.

"What do I owe you?" I ask.

Shit. This is about to get awkward because I just realized I left all my belongings back in the cabin — including my credit cards.

She waves me off. "Christmas World may be a competitor of The Crazy Reindeer, but in this community, we all help one another. A friend of Elias' is a friend of ours."

I smile and wonder just how many "friends" Elias has.

She helps me off the examining table and I rejoin him outside in the biting cold. I'm no longer limping and the scratches don't sting anymore. Elias wasn't wrong about her being good.

"Come on. Let's get away from this shithole," he mumbles, steering me gently to the sleigh. Well, I guess that answers my Elias friendship question, then. Not many friends at all, I imagine.

"But I didn't get to experience Christmas World!" I whine, stopping to a standstill and refusing to move, like a toddler who's had their chocolate Santa taken off them.

"You are too injured to walk around this ghastly place."

"I'm fine. Look." I take a tentative step forward. The throbbing in my ankle has stopped and it doesn't hurt to walk anymore. "See? I'm fine. And I still have one good arm. Let's start over there!" I pull at the sleeve of his coat. "They have a 'Christmas Around the World' Pavilion."

I point at a large attraction full of rides and themed stalls of Christmas food from around the globe. I'm starving and this is foodie Heaven.

"No."

"Please?"

"I said no."

"Pretty please with Christmas fudge on top?" I say in a high voice.

"You are very annoying, you know that?"

"I won't stop begging. Try me. Please please PLEASE!" I clasp my hands together in an am-dram impression of a prayer. "No one likes a killjoy Santa."

"Fine," he grunts. "You have one hour, then I'm going with or without you."

I squeal with delight and am scanning the 'Christmas Around the World' Pavilion, deciding which stall to check out first, when a booming voice rings out in an incongruous Texan accent.

"Well, well, well, this is someone I was *not* expecting to see in my fine establishment!"

It's vape-smoking, monster truck-driving, Mr. Walker. I think of his business card still in my room. This time the tycoon is dressed in a dark blue suit accompanied by a red tie stitched with tiny mistletoe, complete with a sprig of holly in his lapel.

"You're out late," Elias says in perfect English.

"You know what they say," Walker replies. "Christmas never sleeps."

Literally, no one says that.

"You mean money never sleeps," Elias replies, accompanied by a fake grin.

Mr. Walker notices that my arm is in a sling.

"Not another injury, surely?" he says. "That village of yours is unsafe, Elias. My offer still stands. I will give you a good price for the land."

"And I'll give you the same reply I've given you for a year…"

Elias, to my surprise, pauses for dramatic effect, making Mr. Walker frown. "This is the best offer you will get, just take it."

"Why do you even want it?" I blurt out.

They both turn to me in surprise. Walker composes himself as I continue speaking. "No offense," I say to Elias. "You have a lot of land and it's all very pretty, but why there, Mr. Walker? If Elias doesn't want to sell, why not buy elsewhere? I mean, it all looks the same to me. Birch, pine trees, snow and snow, and more snow."

I give a light laugh and the Texan joins in. He pulls a vape out of his pocket and lights it. A fat cigar would suit him better, although the scent of vanilla is more Christmassy, I guess.

"That land is real special, unlike any other in Lapland," he says. He's not lying, he clearly finds it special. "If I were to buy it then it would benefit the entire community. More jobs, fewer accidents."

Not one *ping*. I wish Elias knew of my abilities and I could tell him that this businessman, as showy as he appears to be, doesn't have any bad intentions.

He does, however, have a motive.

"Mr. Walker, you seem very determined to acquire Hullu Poro. You wouldn't be sabotaging Elias' village yourself, would you?"

He laughs, a big hollow laugh like a corny movie villain. "You think *I* have time to go around and mess up this man's electrics, his pipes, cause workplace accidents?"

I know he's being facetious but I drive the point home. My Verity powers are all I have and if he's not behind the destruction then I need to definitely rule him out.

"You haven't answered my question," I say. Walker's face turns hard like stone.

"Listen here, missy. I haven't tampered with his stinkin' village. I don't have the time nor desire to go there and mess things up."

No pings. He's an unpleasant bastard, but he's not lying.

Elias snaps and raises his voice. "But you still want to turn my family business into a giant, vacuous American conglomerate that imports its plastic toys from China." His breaths are coming in sharp rasps and I notice he's put his bunched fist behind his back like he wants to punch the guy in his smug face. I wouldn't blame him if he did. "Don't you worry about my business, Mr. Walker. I'm proud of our little workshop and our Finnish traditions. We don't need you."

"Workshop?" Mr. Walker's eyes narrow. "Oh, of course, those wooden toys your father used to make. I didn't realize you still had the workshop. I guess the local families like to humor you, Elias, because believe me kids today only care about their phones and the latest computer games. They have no use for your antiquated trinkets."

A vein is throbbing in Elias's neck. We better leave. He's about to reply when the door clicks behind us and Dr. Kari steps out of her office.

"Hello, handsome," she says, giving both men a warm smile.

Huh?

Walker wraps his arm around the doctor's waist and plants a slow kiss on her ruby lips. Elias looks away, but not before I notice his cheeks tinge a light pink.

Oh!

OK. Now I get it. This is why he won't sell. The flashy rich American guy got his girl and now he wants his family's land too.

We watch the two of them walk away, Walker's hand on the doctor's hip, her angel wings fluttering in the icy breeze.

"I hope your girlfriend feels better soon," Walker calls out over his shoulder, giving me a too-white smile. Elias doesn't bother responding as he stalks off aggressively in the direction of the Christmas Around the World food stalls.

"Maybe we can find you some sherry, or brandy, or..." I wrack my brain for more Christmas liquor suggestions and spot a stall lit up with brightly-colored bottles. "Spiced gingerbread Irish cream liqueur?"

Elias makes a grunting sound and I'm not sure if it's from disgust or if he's still angry with Walker. Probably both. But walking around seems to be calming him down, and stall by stall he thaws out a little more.

"Try this!" I exclaim through a mouth full of mushy brown stuff. "They're called mince pies but they're not mince as in meat, or mints like minty. I don't get it, but I like it."

Elias tries to dodge my offering and finally succumbs, taking the crumbly pastry from me and chewing it carefully.

"I like it, it's similar to but not as good as my grandmother's Christmas cake. Every year I try to replicate her recipe, but I've never discovered her secret ingredient."

"Is it love?"

"No. I think it's clementine rind."

Right. Well, this British stall is my favorite so far, and I'm not leaving until I've tried every sample the nice lady is handing me.

"What's this?" I ask, pointing at some vegetables.

"Burnt parsnips and potatoes."

I make an unimpressed face. That doesn't sound very interesting. I take a bite — I was wrong.

"What the hell are they cooked in? Damn, they're delicious."

"Goose fat."

I pay the woman for something that she explains is called 'a cracker', although it's not any type of biscuit. It's made of thin card and cylindrical, and when I shake it something rattles.

"Is there candy inside?"

She laughs. "No. You pull it, and it lets out a small bang and there's a toy inside."

These Brits have some weird traditions. I hold one end and signal for Elias to pull the other. He shakes his head, bored of being at this stall for so long.

"Come on, Scrooge McFuck, I only have one working hand."

He rolls his eyes and pulls it, his lips twitching into a smile as something drops to the floor followed by some fluttering paper. It's a gold paper crown and a joke. *Fun!*

I pick them up and clear my throat as I balance the crown on top of my bobble hat. The slip of paper has a Christmas joke written on it.

"Elias, what do you get when you cross a Vampire and a snowman?"

"I don't care."

"It's a Christmas joke, Elias. Play along. What do you get when you cross a Vampire and a snowman?"

He shakes his head and lets out a sigh.

"FROST BITE. Get it?"

He doesn't get it.

He picks up the gift that fell on the ground and studies it. It's a bright green plastic car.

"This is interesting," Elias says, studying the car closely. "These crackers would be a lot more fun if they all contained a quality wooden toy. Imagine each one had a reindeer, a Christmas tree, a little figure of Santa. By the end of the day, the children would have a lovely scene to play with. Something they could bring out every year."

His face lights up for the first time today and I grin, nudging him playfully.

"Is that an actual, real-life, smile? Tell me you're glad we stayed and looked around."

"Shut up and eat your chocolates," he says, handing me a fistful of candy wrapped in different colored cellophane.

"Quality Street," I murmur, popping one in my mouth. "Hmmm, more like Amazing Street."

We eventually move on to other stalls where we try on amusingly cheesy festive jumpers (OK, I do) and I insist that Elias drinks a glass of Coquito, then eggnog, then some hot cider served to us in wooden cups.

"Made from local birch wood," the stall holder tells us.

"I make my own," Elias says, taking a sip.

"Your own wooden cups? From trees?"

"I have a lathe, yes." He straightens my woolly hat, his fingers hovering a second too long by my face. "I'm very good with my hands, you know."

Is Elias flirting with me? Surely not. My, my, Tipsy Elias is a lot more fun than Grumpy Elias. He hiccups and we both start laughing.

"Hey, are you allowed to drink and drive a sleigh?" I ask.

Elias gives me a lopsided grin. "It's no problem as long as the dogs have stayed out of the bar."

Oh, I like Funny Elias.

"Nice to see you get into the Christmas spirit. Literally."

He's doing that staring thing again and this time I feel my cheeks burning.

"So you want to go on some rides?" I ask, pointing at a Ferris wheel shaped like a giant Christmas wreath.

"I feel a bit sick," he says and, now he comes to mention it, I do too. Perhaps mixing roast turkey with sea buckthorn and sherry trifle was not the best idea on top of an adrenaline comedown.

"Yeah. It's been a long day. Let's head back."

The Huskies are excited to see us when we return to the sleigh. They've been waiting for us in a special pen that includes food and water. Who knew Lapland valet parking includes kibble?

I clamber into the sleigh, a bag of Christmas food at my feet. No pain. I must have drunk more than I realize. While Elias calms down the dogs and hooks up the reins I take off my sling and peel the Band-aid off my cut. There's nothing there, not even a scar.

I pull off my boot and feel under my fuzzy socks, no tender skin or swollen ankle either. OK, this is weird. I may be a bit tipsy, but I haven't completely lost my mind. This doesn't make any sense. No injuries go away this fast, unless...

That shimmering balm Dr. Kari treated me with. I *knew* I recognized the smell, and now I know why.

Well, well, well, what do you know? Elias' ex is no angel after all.

She's a Witch.

CHAPTER THIRTEEN

It was cold in my cabin last night and I regretted not asking Elias for some of the reindeer furs from the sleigh, but after some time online I was so exhausted I slept like a yule log.

If it weren't for my phone alarm waking me at eight o'clock in the morning I would presume it was still midnight. How do people function with such a lack of light this time of year?

I'm so desperate for coffee I don't even bother attempting a shower, shrugging on as many layers as I can, and trudging along the large expanse of ankle-deep snow between my cabin and the food hall.

I can't stop thinking about the Witch doctor and her magic potion. Kari must be a Brew Witch. Does Elias know he was banging a Para?

Now I can move both arms I wrap them tightly around me. I didn't think it could possibly get any colder, yet here we are.

I'm nearly at the main building when something catches

my eye. Another animal pen, tucked away behind a big fir tree. This one is not full of dogs though. I march over.

"I have a bone to pick with you," I shout at the big fluffy reindeer. He turns away from me.

"Hello!" I wave my hand and move to the other side of the pen. "I know you understand me, *Fjorn*. We need to talk."

I look around me. Thank God we're alone. If anyone were to see me scolding a reindeer they'd cart me off.

Fjorn sighs, I didn't know reindeer could look disappointed, and walks into his little hut. A few seconds later he re-emerges in human form with a blanket slung around his middle. He looks a bit younger than me, unshaven with wild tangled hair and large deep-brown eyes which remind me of the strong coffee I'm craving.

How is he not cold? He hasn't even got any shoes on. *In the snow!*

"Fine, we can talk," he says. His voice is gravelly, as if he doesn't use it often. "But indoors. I don't want anyone to see me."

Clad in nothing but the blanket he follows me back to my cabin, his bare feet sinking into the snow as if it's warm sand.

"Are you always in the nude?" I ask, glancing pointedly at his pert nipples. Shifters normally retain their clothes during a shift, so he's certainly making a choice here.

"I spend nearly all my time in my reindeer form. I don't need clothes."

He follows me into my crappy cabin and I look around for something to drink. There are some teabags and an old-fashioned kettle, that will do. Fjorn watches me intently the whole time as I find some mugs, and serve up two steaming cups of apple cinnamon tea. I also have some mince pies I brought back from the Christmas market.

I sit opposite him and cross my legs. "So, you're a Shifter?"

"And you're a Witch," he echoes, without missing a beat.

I nod, unsurprised. "You can smell me."

Fjorn adds a ridiculous amount of sugar to his mug but doesn't answer. He doesn't have to. We both know most Paras can smell Witch blood — the only people who can't smell us are other Witches. What I don't understand is why he lives here, in Elias' Christmas village, serving as Santa's single token reindeer. If Elias knows his friend is a reindeer, why would he keep him employed? Does he pay him in moss and ferns?

I don't get why Fjorn would choose this life over one of freedom. Maybe he owes Elias money. Or maybe it's a lot more sinister than that.

The Shifter notices my silence. "You think too much," he says, blowing on his tea.

"Do you know who's messing with the village?"

"No." There's no *ping*. "That's what *you're* here for, isn't it?"

So, he knows I'm a Witch *and* that I'm here to investigate. *Oh!*

"*You're* the one who gave the tipoff to The Blood Web Chronicle?"

"I did." He nods, his movements reindeer-like as if his head were heavier than it is.

"Where are your...?" I gesture vaguely around the crown of my head searching for the word. "Antlers. I noticed you don't have any."

"Male reindeer lose them in the winter. We fight with them, they grow back in the spring. Female reindeer are the only deer to have antlers this time of year, you know."

"So Santa's reindeer are all female?"

He laughs and nods. Of course, they are. Santa's male reindeer would probably get a bout of man flu on the busiest night of the year and demand the night off.

"Isn't it weird having things sticking out of your body?" I ask.

"What's it like having *those*?" he tilts the teacup in the direction of my breasts.

"Heavy, inconvenient, yet at times totally awesome."

"Ditto," he says, pointing a finger at his head.

"You haven't even finished your tea and you're already bringing up my boobs?" I tease. "I know you saw me naked in the window the other day. Is that what you do, perve on all the female guests?"

I wonder how many women he talks to. How much human interaction he gets, aside from Elias…who isn't exactly the chattiest of people.

"I'm afraid you're not my type," Fjorn says with a smirk.

"Not enough…"

"Big, thick, fighting antlers," Fjorn finishes, and we both laugh. I'm surprised he's friends with Elias. Maybe Fjorn has enough personality for the two of them.

"So, if it's men you like, are you and Elias…"

"No. I believe you already met his type. I saw you heading back from Christmas World."

"Yeah, Dr. Kari. I presume you're aware she's a Witch, seeing as you can smell our kind a mile away."

He gives a slow nod and I lean forward.

"Do you think it's her? Do you think she could be the one messing with the village? Cursing it somehow?"

"The doctor doesn't have a single bad bone in her body."

No *ping*. Kari the angel.

"If you say so."

"She's harmless." He takes another sip of his tea. "You know you're his type too, right?"

I snort-laugh. "Elias? Pffft! He can't stand me. I don't think he can stand anyone if I'm honest. Except you, maybe."

"Elias is in a great deal of pain."

"What do you mean?"

The reindeer falls silent. Stupid me, thinking Fjorn would ever tell me anything personal about his friend. He hasn't told me one untruth. Fjorn may be a Shifter of few words but at least every one of them is pure and honest.

"Do you have any suspicions about the village? Anything that may help me?" I ask, pushing a mince pie in his direction. I planned to take my stash of goodies from last night's market back to New York and Jackson, but at this rate, I will have eaten them all by Christmas Day. Fjorn takes the little pie and bows his head gratefully; another reindeer habit.

"I've been trying to figure it out for months. The human police are little help. The animals in the forest don't know much either."

"You can communicate with them?"

"In a way. I pick up on fear and scents. Sometimes there's a lot of fear in the air, here and in the forest. I've picked up strange smells and seen tracks in the snow that instantly disappear. I've never been able to follow them, though."

"Do you think whatever bit me yesterday is what's causing the chaos? I could feel and hear them, but I couldn't see anything."

Last night I searched the Blood Web for hours, but apart from a few isolated incidents of vandalism that turned out to be disgruntled Werewolf cubs, there are no records of Paranormals that can make themselves invisible. Even thinking of all of this as a curse is a stretch. A haunting, however, is quite possible. There are many records of ghosts remaining unseen, although their tricks are normally more bloody and less petty.

"There's definitely some kind of magic afoot," Fjorn agrees. "But I haven't been able to discover it. Can't you use your Witchy magic to discover the cause?"

"I'm using my Witchy magic right now."

I brace myself for the look of disappointment but Fjorn only nods. "A Verity Witch reporter. Makes sense."

Does it? Perhaps if I were a stronger Witch I could cast a spell to catch the perpetrator and not have to settle for questioning Elias' reindeer friend.

"When did you move here? I know nothing about reindeer habits. Like, do you have a pack or something?"

He shakes his head in that slow way of his again, his tangled hair looking a lot like the shaggy fur around his reindeer neck.

"It's a herd, and no, I don't have anyone. I left my old life long ago for the forests of Lapland. For freedom. Elias discovered me one day, wounded from a fight. I guess my antlers aren't as strong as that of an older reindeer. He nursed me back to health with the help of Dr. Kari's fancy potions, and that's how he discovered I was a Shifter."

Shifters turn back to their animal form when they die. Fjorn must have been in really bad shape if he'd been unable to control his shifts.

"Was Elias shocked? Few humans are aware of our world."

Fjorn gives me a thin smile and shrugs.

"The veil is thinner this far north, especially in Lapland. Humans here are spiritual, they understand nature. You've seen this place. It's hard not to believe in magic when you live here."

I nod, wondering how long I can keep my secret from Elias. Would it be easier if I told him the truth? Maybe he'll be cool about me being a Witch.

"Does Elias know about Kari?" I ask.

Fjorn shakes his head. "No. They weren't together that long. She's a girl who likes the pretty things in life and believe me when I say this place gets less and less pretty every day." I'm not entirely sure he respects the beautiful doctor, even if she *is* sweet and good at helping people. I don't know why that makes me happy, but it does. "Anyway, when Elias' village went bankrupt he had to sell all of his reindeer. I used to visit him often, and when I found out I offered to help him through the winter season. I owe him a debt of gratitude for saving my life."

We both sit in silence for a while. I think about Elias having to sell his reindeer, about living out here all alone, everything he's ever worked for slowly slipping between his fingers.

"What type of Paranormals live around here?" I ask.

"I don't really know. A few errant Shifters here and there, Kari, and a Vampire that went on a bloody rampage a few years back. The locals blamed wild wolves."

That's not much to go on. Fjorn strikes me as one of those people you'd find living in a van alone in the middle of nowhere.

"Well, since you don't have your hooves on the Para pulse, do you know who does? Who I can question? Elias isn't exactly open-minded or much of a chatterbox."

"There is *someone* who knows about all the magic in these parts, someone I haven't been able to get to. But…"

His cautious tone instantly sets me on edge.

"Why haven't you been able to get to them?"

"I got close and she tried to drown me."

She tried to drown me…

"Ugh, for fucks sake!" I lean back in my chair with dramatic exasperation. I know exactly what he's talking about and there's nothing I hate more than Sirens.

"I'm not immune to a Siren's song, you know," I say. "I'll drown too."

I try to blink away the horrifying memories of being kidnapped by a bunch of them last spring, subsequently blowing up their Californian nest.

"I heard this one doesn't drown women. Especially…"

"Especially what?"

"Especially if you bring her some jam."

Jam? What sort of Into the Woods bullshit is this?

"Wonderful," I huff into the dregs of my tea. "I'll just grab some Strawberry Bonne Maman and my waterproof boots and hope the scaly bitch doesn't drown me."

CHAPTER FOURTEEN

T he ice cracks and fans out beneath my snow boots like spider silk as I take one more careful step toward the center of the lake.

Why am I doing this again? I don't want to join in any reindeer games. If I end up cryogenically frozen listening to Finnish Ariel and her warbling bullshit for all of eternity I'm going to add myself to the list of people who are haunting Elias.

I brush the snow away from the thick icy ground and knock on it hard.

"Hello! Anybody home? Do you have a moment to talk about our Lord and savior, Poseidon?"

God, I hope these Mermaids like sass, 'cause that's all I've got. That and three jars of fucking jam.

The sooner I get this over with, the better. Fjorn told me multiple Mermaids dwell in the larger lakes across Lapland — Arctic Mermaids who go by many names including the Nixie and the Näkki. Like any animal or the human race, Paranormals can appear very differently depending on where they live and their habitats. By all accounts, these are not like the surfer dudes I've encountered in the past.

Fjorn said the Näkki are viscous and violent and like to gossip, but that I'd be safe as they only drown men because they live in all-female hives. Well, that's nice, at least I don't have to deal with more horny Mermen.

I take another step across the thick ice, brushing away the snow with my foot as I go. I can't make out where this lake starts and where it ends, but I'm pretty certain I'm somewhere close to the middle now. I get down on all fours and peer through the ice.

"Hey!" I knock again. "Anyone there?"

A shadow passes below me, and I scuttle back.

Fuck!

It's one thing to come looking for Merfolk, but it's another to have them swimming beneath your feet like a school of hungry sharks. I glance back. There's nothing for miles but white snow and black woods. Fjorn dropped me off at a safe distance, far away enough that he wouldn't hear the Siren song. Or my screams, should anything go wrong.

I'm all alone out here — no houses, no cars, no people. Just me and my jam.

The ice gives way a little and I jump back as cracks start to Etch A Sketch their way along the ice. I feel a presence stir beneath me and I hold my breath. One more crack erupts beneath the weight of my foot, sprouting like a bolt of lightning across the sky.

I peer closer to the ground and let out a yelp as I'm met with a face pressed up against the ice. With long tapering fingers splayed out against the glass, the Mermaid stares up at me like a child pressing her sticky mouth against a shop window.

"Hey there…" I say softly like I'm trying to calm her into not eating me.

I wait. She stares. All is silent but for the howl of the wind and the shifting of the ice. Then she bangs her clawed hands against the ice with a resounding crack and I scuttle backward. But I'm not fast enough as something closes tightly around my ankle, digging its sharp talons into my flesh.

I let out a scream. A scream I know no one can hear.

Her hold around my leg pulls me and I fall back, my head smashing against the ice, as she begins to drag me along the frozen lake. I try and sit up, see where she's taking me, but there's nothing ahead but snow and ice and…a gaping huge hole that has suddenly appeared, the water beneath black as ink.

I flail around, my fingertips trying to find purchase on the snow but I'm unable to grab at anything that will stop me from sliding towards the freezing cold water and my imminent death.

"Stop!" I shout. "I come in peace!"

How the fuck are you supposed to greet Merpeople?

My head is bouncing along the lake's hard icy surface, my ears grazing along the cold and filling with snow. I kick out but I can't see the face of the creature dragging me along the ice.

"I have a gift for you!" I cry out.

The Siren stops dragging me, leaving my foot suspended inches over the sloshing water. Inches from being submerged in its freezing depths.

I scramble backward and get to my feet, brushing myself off. Then I see her. A beautiful woman is floating waist-high in the hole in the lake's icy surface, resting her elbows over the edge like she's at a hotel pool waiting for a *Mer*tini.

Her hair is so blonde it's virtually white, cascading down her back like rippling satin. Her cheekbones are high, her eyes clear as ice, and her bare breasts bob on the water's surface. She crooks a finger at me, and I step closer. I can't help it. I *have* to get closer to her.

I crouch down and hold out a hand. I need to touch her. I need to feel her soft skin against the tips of my fingers, her lips on mine, her body pressed against me as we sink deeper and deeper into the enveloping abyss.

As my face nears hers, she sniffs the air, her wet hair glistening in the weak light, then slowly her features begin to change. Her eyes go from round and clear to black slits, her face drains of color until it's practically translucent, and her fingers grow long and thin like dead twigs, her hooked nails sharp as talons.

"Witch," she says.

Her magic over me snaps away and I stumble backward, leaving at least six feet between us. *Fuck.* I'd forgotten the power Sirens can have. Did I learn nothing in LA?

"I… I brought you…" I hold out my bag, cold and fear and the remnants of her magic have me stammering like a fool.

"Gift?" she lisps, her lips two thin lines against her gelatinous face. She holds her hands out, like two spindly starfish trying to grab at the bag on my shoulder. "Give me my gift!"

I shake my head and square my shoulders. *Enough of this shit!*

"You will get your present when you help me with my questions," I shout, feeling absolutely ridiculous that I'm standing in the middle of the lake arguing with a fish.

The Näkki Mermaid moves her head from side to side like an eel, swaying in the icy water.

"One question. One answer," she says.

Right. One question. I need to think about this one carefully. Where do I start? I want to ask about local Paranormal creatures, who's behind the Hullu Poro destruction, what their beef is, what's so special about Elias' land, and what has happened to his absent dad, and I wonder if she knows the recipe for those rice pudding pastry things.

She's tapping her sharp nails on the ice, her slitty mouth pursing with impatience.

I clear my throat and clasp my bag to me tighter. "Here's my question. What kind of Paranormal creatures are trying to destroy The Crazy Reindeer Christmas village and why?"

She tips her head to one side, her long hair flowing around her in the water. "I said just one question."

"OK. Chill." I take a deep breath. "Just tell me what's destroying The Crazy Reindeer Christmas Village. I know it's something non-human, but what?"

The Näkki hums softly, swaying back and forth as if she's considering her answer. Shapes and shadows shift beneath the ice at my feet, and I wonder how many more of these translucent Mermaids are swimming about underneath me. I shiver as I shuffle from foot to foot, willing her to give me an answer already so I can stop standing in the middle of a fucking lake.

Jesus, what's taking her so long? Is she secretly Googling the answer on her shellphone?

When she finally starts to speak her voice is a melodic rasp, the sound of waves lapping at the shore and shingly stones shifting in the waves.

You cannot see
The help unseen,
A master stays unheard.
Listen closely and you'll find
Their manners mean
His song absurd.
Greatest of all time
Bringer of shiny things
Beneath the ancient stone

For him their filthy song still rings.

That's it? That's her answer? What in the name of fortune cookies is that riddled nonsense?

"My gift," she says, holding out her hand.

"Listen nautical Nostradamus, that was bullshit. Give me some real information."

"My gift," she screeches, making my ears ring. In one swift motion, she hauls herself out of the water, sliding along the ice like an emaciated seal in a wig, her sharp-clawed nails pulling her along the ice. I stagger backward but she's fast, slithering towards me, her pointed teeth bared. "My gift!"

"All right, all right," I shout, my hands held out like a stop sign. She freezes. I rummage around inside my bag, wondering how fast a slimy Mermaid can jump at my throat if she's not fond of my choice of jam flavor.

Carefully I take out a glass jar and a silver spoon.

"Here," I hold them out to her.

She slides back into her hole again and sinks beneath the surface. Does she not want her sugary gift, then? For a second, I think I'm free and consider turning back, but then her head pops out again and she leans against the rim.

"What kind of jam did you bring?"

"Seriously? Beggars can't be choosers," I mumble, reading the handwritten label. I wonder if Elias made this, or maybe his mother did. She looks like the jam-making kind.

The Mermaid starts to screech like a seagull trapped in a trashcan, her spindly fingers grasping for the jar in my hand.

"OK, OK, chill! It's berries!" I shout, squinting at the label and trying to decipher Elias's handwriting. "Bilberries and cloudberries. Homemade. It's sweet and tastes like autumn and honey and…take it."

I open the jar and slide it across the ice along with the

spoon. Mermaids like spoons, right? I mean, Ariel had loads of them and brushed her hair with a fork.

The Näkki twists her head this way and that, then smells the jar, dipping one of her talons into the jam. A thin, black tongue slithers out of her slitty mouth and touches the jelly. I hold my breath. Then with a sharp sudden motion, she plunges her entire hand into the pot and smears it over her translucent face.

"More jam," she cries, throwing the empty glass jar aside. "More jam. More jam!"

I only have two more jars in my bag. Why didn't I take more? Elias has loads of pots in his pantry. Lingonberry, raspberry, blackberry, I'm sure there was even one called fucking starlitskyberry. I should have taken them all!

I take a step back, and another, the ice creaking loudly beneath my boots while dark shadows congregate under the ice. Great, now I'm going to drown because this Mermaid wasn't ready for my jelly. I throw the second jar at her and she snatches it with inhumane speed.

The Nåkki scoops fistfuls of bilberry jam into her mouth, making a noise like a blocked drain as she slurps it off her fingers, her other hand clawing at her sisters who have been alerted to my berry-licious gift by her gluttonous cries of pleasure. The other Mermaids push their way up, squeezing through the hole and cracking its surface, the chasm splitting the ice and making it wobble beneath me.

One jumps out of the hole, followed by another. They flop on to the lake's hard surface, slick and terrifying, their collective weight causing the ice to buckle. I try to run back to land but my snow boots have no grip and I'm flailing on the spot. As more Mermaids clamber onto the ice it breaks away, one end tilting up to the gray sky and the other end sinking into the water. I'm sliding, running on the spot, and am forced to launch myself onto another floating piece of ice. I'm on all fours, trying to gain enough balance to stand, when a Mermaid swipes at me, her sharp talons piercing fabric and flesh.

My bag slips off my shoulder and slides away. There's still one more jar left in there. It may be the only thing standing between me and a watery grave.

"Jam," croaks another Mermaid, this time larger and toothier. Iridescent red scales glow on the back of her hands as she belly crawls towards me like *Free Willy* meets *The Ring.*

Fuck! I need to get to my bag.

Three creatures are closing in on me, all of them shimmering and dangerous, their bodies making a swooshing sound as they haul their slimy balk in my direction.

"Jam. Jam. Jam," they chant.

They haven't noticed I don't have my bag. I have to get to it and lure them away before they drag me into the water. I make a quick calculation and decide to go for it. If I throw myself along the ice, I may be able to do this, I may just make it to land in one piece. Because if I don't get away from these preserve-loving Sirens soon, *I'm* the one who's going to be preserved.

Taking a deep breath, I run at the group of Mermaids, and just as their hands reach out for me I throw myself onto my stomach and slide headfirst toward land...and my bag.

Delving inside I pull out the last jam jar and throw it as far from me as I can. It rolls, and rolls until it reaches a hole in the ice and plops into the water. They all dive in after it and I take my chance. Jumping one final time across a stretch of water, I hit the last solid piece of ice attached to the land and run.

The ice has turned a multitude of colors as dozens of Mermaids slither and clamber for the last of the jam in the water. With every one of my footsteps, combined with the Näkki's bodies pushing against the ice, the surface beneath me starts to crack. Twice my foot falls into the water and I pull it out just in time as hands clasp for me and voices screech.

Even once I'm on land I don't stop running, snow covering my knees and soaking my legs, every breath freezing in my lungs like ice cubes.

I find Fjorn hidden behind a tree in his reindeer form, waiting.

He shifts, this time wearing warm clothes.

"Any luck?" he says, as the manic call of the Sirens continues to ring in my ears like a fire drill.

"One useless riddle," I say, panting. "But thanks a lot for ruining jam for me."

CHAPTER FIFTEEN

I haven't been able to track Elias down all day, but after lunch, I find him at the front of the main building hanging little golden bells and straw decorations on the fir tree outside. I haven't told him about the Mermaids yet and their riddle, which Fjorn and I have spent hours trying to crack, but it still makes no sense.

There's no point asking Elias, though. He's already refused to talk to me about the fact his best friend is a reindeer, so I doubt he's ready for the 'there are Merfolk out there too' talk.

"What are you doing?" I ask instead.

The decorations are a bit Blair Witch Project for my liking, but he's concentrating hard so I figured it's a tradition of some sort.

"It's for the Yule Goat," he says.

The what now?

I can't help laughing, but as usual Elias' face is nothing but pure exasperation.

"Remember the goat-man stories the elders at the workshop were telling you about? Hanging the decorations up is a pointless custom my father has always insisted we do year after year, since I was a small child. These ornaments and other shiny offerings are meant to ward off the original Joulupukki. The bells are meant to keep harm away, and the ornaments are a type of bribe. You put them up each year and on Christmas Eve they disappear. They say the goat-man takes them and in exchange brings you good luck for the following year. It's silly. It's not like we've had any good luck anyway."

"We really need to talk about…"

He shakes his head. "I have more Santa duties in an hour."

I get it. He's not a big talker. But neither am I going to get anywhere with this riddle on my own.

"OK. Later," I say, heading back to reception. Elias plants himself in my way and picks up a sack by his feet.

"Is that full of presents?" I cry out in mock glee. "For me? You're so kind!"

He shakes his head. "The Elf is sick, my mother had to go to Helsinki for an emergency, and Fjorn has a check-up."

"At the vet?" I grin.

He rolls his eyes, although I'm not sure what any of this has to do with his bulging bag.

I press past him towards a cookie bar I just noticed. Elias follows me inside, scowling as I help myself to a gingerbread.

"The show will be incomplete."

"Oh no, Elias. Who will help depress all the little children now?" I tease, snickering inwardly at how easy it is to make him mad.

"You," he grunts, throwing the sack at me. "*You* will depress them."

What? Stumbling forward I grab the sack with one hand, peer inside, look up at his smug face, and look inside again. What in the Jingle Jangle is this?

I pull out what appears to be a jumble of rags and white fur and hold it out to Elias.

"What the hell is this?"

"It's an Elf costume."

I delve inside the bag deeper, pulling out a few more items.

"Stripy stockings? A Santa hat? These items don't even match."

"I told you, our costume room burned down. This is the best I could gather together. The children don't care. I just need an assistant."

"No way," I moan through a mouthful of crumbly cookies. I pass him back the sack, but he shoves it in my hand with another grunt.

"It's happening."

"You think this raggedy thing is going to bring festive joy to the lives of innocent children?" I say, inspecting the tattered excuse for an outfit in my hand. "Not even a zombie Santa would wear this."

I thrust the Elf top in the air. "This isn't Elf on the shelf, this is do-it-yourself Elf. Broken sewing machine Elf. Needs some financial help Elf."

"I get it!"

Elias' face falls and I feel a pang of guilt. I think back to what Fjorn said about him having to sell everything to get through the winter season. How can I do this to a man with only half a reindeer to his name?

"Fine. Give me a minute," I say, holding up one finger. "Accessories can save anything."

Lucky for Elias I'm not great at capsule wardrobes and I always pack more than I need. Thinking of the red velvet dress still in my suitcase, I rush back to my room and study the sad excuse for a costume Elias just handed me.

It's even worse than the outfit Elias' mom was wearing. At

times like these, I wish I were more than just a Verity Witch and had the amazing sewing abilities Silkmage Witches have.

It's fine. I think I can still rescue it. Turning flea market finds into chic outfits has become a bit of a hobby of mine since moving to New York, where eating and clothing are mutually exclusive on a Blood Web Chronicles salary.

There are scissors in the small kitchen and I have one of those free mini sewing kits I once got from a hotel room stashed among the trash in my purse.

I slip on the long red and white striped stockings, and the Santa hat is borderline acceptable, but the rest is going to have to go. I don't mind sacrificing my red dress if it means saving myself from public yuletide humiliation.

I snip off the white fur from whatever the hell the outfit is meant to be and add it to the belled sleeves of my velvet dress. The dress is short so I turn it into more of a leotard — there's no point having cute stockings if you can't see them.

OK, this looks a lot better. Coupled with long white gloves found at the bottom of the sack and the thick black belt I have in my suitcase, I've instantly gone from Creepy Clause to Santa's favorite hoe hoe hoe.

I adjust my hair and makeup and place the fur-trimmed hat on my head at a jaunty angle.

Back outside I instantly regret having added heeled boots to my ensemble as I wade through the thick snow to the main building — thank god my ankle is no longer hurting.

Families are making their way to the front entrance. Without them seeing, I slip through the back door to the large hall which is decked out with Christmas trees and the Santa throne again, minus Fjorn the reindeer this time.

Fresh holly hangs from the ceiling that's now decorated with more straw ornaments and shiny bells. There are also decorated birch branches, pine centerpieces, and stacked logs adding more Scandi glory to the dining hall.

Elias has clearly been in the woods, sourcing, and chopping. Though when he has the time, I do not know. I wave away thoughts of Elias chopping wood in the twilight. No one needs that mental image.

If his Christmas village business doesn't work out he'd make a great Ikea seasonal set designer. I should tell him, but I'm afraid I'm one insult away from him turning me into blood dumpling soup.

There's even a giant handmade candy cane leaning against a table full of small colorful parcels. The little light there was in the day has now dimmed to night, the twinkly lights strung around the room casting a soft golden glow.

Elias has his back to me sorting through the tiny parcels, which I realize are individually wrapped cookies for the children.

He must have heard me come in but keeps his back to me. "Take these," he says, picking up the tray of cookies.

Something in my chest aches at the thought of him in the kitchen individually wrapping each cookie and tying a bow on them. Does this man ever sleep?

I accept the tray but he still hasn't turned around.

"All you need to do is take a photo of me and the child using that Polaroid camera over there, then give them the photo and cookie as they leave. That's their gift. Doors open in three minutes."

I nod silently.

"Was that clear?" he asks, reaching for another tray of cookies to hand to me.

He turns around and the creases of his usually furrowed brow instantly disappear as he takes in my altered ensemble. In the soft light of the room, he looks almost calm, almost at peace. Then his face starts to change from incomprehension to surprise, his mouth opening and closing like he's not sure what to say.

"I hope you don't mind that I adjusted the costume a little," I say, twirling on the spot.

The tray in Elias' hand starts to teeter to one side and I lean forward to catch it, my fingers folding over his. I take the tray off him, biting back a smile as he looks anywhere but at me.

"You will be cold," he says.

"But I'm wearing fur," I say, showing him my draping long sleeves. "See?"

His gaze flickers from my face to the gap between the top of my stockings and the hem of my velvety leotard.

"Put the cookies over there by the exit."

I place them on the table beside the giant candy cane, making sure to give Elias a good view of my velvet-clad ass.

When I turn back around he turns away and I try not to laugh that I caught him looking at me. A bit of fun will do this icy guy some good. He needs to thaw out a little.

"Are you blushing, Elias?"

"Go," he says, clearing his throat and nodding towards the door. "The children will be here soon."

I ignore him.

"You look nice too," I reply. I'm not lying. He's made more effort than last time, both with the room and his outfit, even though his suit is still straining around his strong arms.

There are more families than yesterday. I'm losing track of the days but I think tomorrow is Christmas Eve.

"Wow!" one of the mothers says to her son in the stroller. "Look at the pretty lights and Santa's pretty assistant."

No *ping*. People genuinely like the effort we've made.

I catch Elias' eye and he gives me a small smile, filling me with relief. I was worried I'd gone a bit too far with this outfit but it's clearly better than the drunken Elf he had helping him yesterday.

I accompany each child to Elias and take their photo, it's repetitive but it's worth it to see their faces light up as he asks them what they want for Christmas.

Weirdly, I'm glad I agreed to help. I'm actually enjoying myself. I'm basically doing community service, like a human treetop angel. As I'm internally praising myself I catch Elias watching me.

He seems happier being Santa today, a little calmer than yesterday. It's nice to see him get a few hours' break from the stress his business has been causing him.

Life would be a lot easier for him if he just sold this place, but I know more than anyone that letting go of the past is hard. Especially when it has to do with family.

"Can I take a photo of the four of you?" a woman asks, as her two daughters shuffle up beside me and Elias.

"Get closer," she says.

I perch on the arm of the throne and Elias has to hook his hand around my waist to keep me steady. My arms and legs are getting cold but his hand is like a scorching hot patch on my side. I lean closer to him and place a hand on his shoulder to stop myself from wobbling. His body stiffens beneath my palm, and then he relaxes as if we're the perfect festive family.

He's staring straight into the camera and I plaster on a smile, but I can tell he can feel me looking at him.

"Am I making you nervous?" I whisper.

"Of course not."

Ping. I keep grinning as a few other parents ask to take photos with their children scattered around us.

"Santa's girlfriend is beautiful," one little girl shouts out.

"She doesn't look like any Mrs. Claus I've seen before," mutters one of the dads, eyeing me up and down.

His wife nudges him and urges their kids towards the table where the cookie gifts are waiting.

"Maybe she's just Santa's friend. Or...sister."

Although Elias doesn't look at me I can see his lips twitching in amusement.

Another mom takes a photo and he tightens his grasp at my waist.

"Don't forget the gifts," he says, and I realize he's talking to me.

I clamber off the throne and go back to my cookie-handing-out duties, wondering just how much longer I'm expected to stand in these heels. Just as I think the line is dwindling, more families turn up.

"And what would you like for Christmas, young man?" Elias asks the next child softly.

The little boy standing before him looks about six years old. He's missing a front tooth, and he whistles as he talks. He clambers onto Elias' lap, but instead of looking excited like the other kids, his face is full of concern.

"Some people say you aren't real, but I believe in you, Santa."

Elias smiles at the boy, his frosty blue eyes twinkling in a way I've not seen before. "Believing is its own kind of magic," he says gently. "And Christmas is all about magic. What toys would you like me to bring you this year?"

The boy lowers his voice to a whisper. "I don't want any toys for Christmas...because..."

Elias waits patiently and I bite my lips together, waiting.

"Because I don't want to play alone. Can you use your magic to find me some friends?"

"We just moved here," the mother explains awkwardly.

A lump has formed in my throat, but Elias remains calm.

"Of course I will make sure you have friends as long as

you believe that you will find them. And you can come here to play with our Huskies any time."

The boy beams back at him and gives him a hug, and I smile extra wide as I hand him two cookies instead of one.

I go to smile at Elias but he's pointing at the Polaroid camera on the table beside me. "Photo first, then the gift," he barks, shattering the warm and fuzzies inside of me in an instant.

I do as I'm told, and the rest of the afternoon goes by in a blur of cookies, cameras, and Elias being his usual grouchy self.

I guess Christmas magic only applies to children.

CHAPTER SIXTEEN

I trudge back to my cabin through the snow, pissed that Elias didn't even say thank you for helping him with his Santa duties or for sweeping up the piles of colorful tissue paper that the children had thrown to the floor, in their eagerness to eat their cookies.

My feet throb, my throat aches from calling out "next", and I have blisters all over my toes. Who knew smiling at children would be so exhausting?

Cradling another cup of tea, I plop myself into the armchair and stretch my legs. Even taking off this stupid velvet outfit is too much effort right now. A howling wind has picked up outside and snow is whipping against the window.

Elias has fixed the electricity and brought me a heater, which is now warm by my feet. But the outside chill is creeping under the door and through the drafty windows, seeping into my bones. I grab a blanket and bundle up in it, gazing at the flurry of snow out the window. One of the few village street lamps that work illuminates the fields outside, which look like a sheet of melting marshmallows. The snowfall has picked up intensely, reminding me of that blizzard in the forest yesterday.

The lights in my room flicker, casting shadows on the walls, and I pick up a book I bought with me. Another light flickers. And another one. Then the lights go out entirely.

"Fuck!"

Scrambling off the couch I curse as I knock over the trash can, stubbing my toe and hobbling on one leg.

I remember an old dusty flashlight in one of the kitchen drawers. Stumbling about blindly I manage to locate it, hoping the batteries work. They do, but they must be close to running out because the light is faint.

There has to be a fuse box here somewhere. Using the flashlight, and still trying to keep the blanket around my shoulders, I search for the power outlet trying one switch at a time, nervous about being electrocuted again.

Click. Click. *Nada.*

I sweep the light from one corner of the cabin to another. There's a bundle of string along the wall and I crouch down and pick it up, squinting against the weak light of the flashlight. It's not string, it's cables, and each one has been shredded and chewed through again.

Fuck this and fuck the Merbitch who couldn't give me a straight answer. I clamber back onto the couch and curl up into a ball, too cold to deal with all of this by myself.

My phone only has 6% battery left and there's no WiFi — not that I have any emergency cabin repairs number to call. I pull the blankets up higher around my neck. God, I'm so fucking cold.

I really need to get changed out of this stupid costume and into some warm clothes. I get up and head for my bed where my suitcase is, just as the batteries of the flashlight turn off. It's pitch dark now and I have no idea where anything is.

Shit!

I bury myself under the duvet, and will myself to fall asleep until the morning.

Half an hour later and I'm wide awake, shaking like a frost-covered leaf. Not only am I too cold to sleep but I'm also far too angry. I can't stop thinking about Elias and how he kept swinging from hot to cold with me this afternoon. How he couldn't even thank me for doing him a favor when he has me staying in a cryo chamber!

My whole body shakes with cold, my teeth chattering uncontrollably.

Oh my lord, how can it be this freezing? It's unnatural. I wonder if Fjorn gets cold too. Reindeer skin is thick. He's probably gallivanting through snow dunes right now, having the time of his life with all his other reindeer friends.

That's it. I can't do this. Elias will just have to fix the power. Again. I'm not exactly enamored by the idea of talking to the grumpy asshole past bedtime, but I have no choice.

I grapple around for my clothes and coat, but it's so dark I can't tell what's what. All I can feel are sequins and heels. Where the hell are my warm clothes?!

My snow boots are by the door so I wrap the blankets around me reindeer Shifter style, pull on my fleece-lined boots, and step outside, the door slamming with a flurry of snow behind me.

Shit. My key!

Doesn't matter, Elias will have one, I think, as I wade through the snowy tundra separating my cabin from his.

His mini house still looks as pretty as when I first saw it, no wonder he kept the best one for himself. It's lit up with blissful light and heat, and even has cute lights around the window. His cabin is also at least double the size of mine.

I knock on the door, already sopping wet and frozen to the bone. The snow is falling so fast I can't even blink easily, and it's already gathering on my blankets.

After three more bangs, Elias finally opens the door. He's still clad in his Santa pants and fur-trimmed Santa coat, but beneath it all he's shirtless. Rows of muscle ripple and flex along his abdomen as he swigs from the neck of a bottle of beer.

"Why are you half naked?" I exclaim.

"I could ask you the same thing."

"I'm wearing blankets. You're the one who looks like you're about to host a Christmas bachelorette party."

"How humorous," he says, buttoning up his coat. "You know, you're not quite as funny as you think you are."

How fucking dare he? I'm hilarious!

"Yeah, well maybe my big-city humor doesn't translate well to the village. Anyway, my power is out."

"And?"

"What do you mean *and*?!" I howl. "I've been working for you all afternoon and this is the thanks I get? Go fucking fix it."

"Can't." Elias takes another lazy swig of beer as if he has all the time in the world to watch me get hypothermia.

"Of course, you can! You're the manager, front desk staff, owner of the village, and even Santa himself. It's YOUR job to fix the power."

"We need to wait until tomorrow when there's more light and the storm calms down."

I sigh, brushing snow from my blankets and shivering. "This is the least fun Christmas I've ever had."

Something twitches in his cheek. "No one said Christmas is meant to be fun."

Literally, everyone says that.

"Maybe you shouldn't be a Santa if you hate Christmas!" I say. My voice rising with each word.

"WELL MAYBE YOU SHOULDN'T COME TO LAPLAND IF YOU HATE SNOW!" he thunders back.

I gesture at my knees. "I like snow, I just don't like being buried alive in it."

His brow briefly creases as he glances at the space between the top of my stockings and the trim of my leotard.

"Everything you do is so inappropriate. Such a drama queen. All you Americans, such drama queens!"

"And you're nothing but a cold-hearted Grinch who cares about no one but himself!"

This time he doesn't bother to reply, simply stepping back into his cabin and slamming the door behind him.

I'm standing there, my mouth gaping in shock when a pile of snow gathering on the top of his door falls on my head. I scream and he opens the door again, glaring at me standing there like a half-defrosted snowman.

"You will wake the reindeer," he hisses. Then slams the door again.

"You only have one fucking reindeer!" I holler back. "And you're probably going to turn Fjorn into soup too!"

Elias opens the door again. This time his eyes scan me up and down like he's only just realized I'm soaking wet and not going anywhere.

"Fine. Come in."

CHAPTER SEVENTEEN

My teeth chatter as I follow Elias inside to the fire-lit cabin, fingers and toes instantly tingling as the heat of the room thaws my ice-cold skin. His house is exactly how I expected it to be, but nicer. Much nicer. There are antlers on the rough log walls, a roaring fire in a stone hearth, an old-fashioned Aga stove in the corner, and sheepskin rugs on the floor. Above me is a mezzanine level, like the one the workshop had, where I can make out a large double bed covered in knitted throws.

"Strip," he says.

I make a face of disgust and he sighs deeply.

"For the sauna."

"Hah!" I laugh. "You wish."

Elias throws me another disgruntled look, rinsing the last dregs from his bottle of beer and putting it down. "Trust me, I would rather eat spruce needles than see you naked."

Ping.

Ha!

"The sauna is the fastest way to get warm. Most Finnish

country homes have them. It's not the fancy luxury you Americans think it is."

"Is that why you're walking like that? Because you were about to have a Santa solo sauna?" I scoff.

"I was already naked in the sauna when you knocked on the door. I put the pants and jacket on to see who it was."

Oh.

He opens a wooden door at the back of the room and I take in the small room with its slatted pine benches and wooden bucket with a rope handle. The scent of birch fills the room. Who has a fucking sauna in their living room? OK, the Finnish do. He just told me. But still. It's all very over the top.

A thought suddenly hits me. "Did you build this yourself?"

"Of course I did. I built my entire cabin."

Of course he did.

I wrap my sodden blanket around me tighter, although I have to admit the idea of a warm sauna is tantalizing. But not like this. Saunas are something I would normally do with my friends in Ktown, followed by herbal tea and gossip, not squished in some Scandi broom cupboard with a miserable innkeeper judging me.

I reluctantly peel away the layers of snow-soaked blankets, hand them to him, and stand there in my ridiculously skimpy Santa's sexy helper outfit. This outfit looks so much more suggestive now it's completely wet and we're alone in his house.

"You can't come in there with me," I say, pointing at the steamy room.

"As I said, I'd rather eat spruce needles."

Liar.

"For all I know, spiky fir trees are a Finnish delicacy."

Elias rolls his eyes and hands me a towel. I take it and

hide from view in the kitchen, reluctantly peeling off my costume while keeping my bra and panties on beneath the towel. I squeeze into the sauna where Elias has already begun to pour water over the bright red coals in the corner. It really is a sauna for one — or, at least, two people who actually like one another.

"What's that?" I ask, pointing at a bundle of leaves tied with string beside the hot stones.

"It's birch leaves. We use them to whip our hot skin while in here," he replies.

I laugh. "Calm down, kinky Claus."

He huffs, his gaze settling on the tops of my legs. "Why do you still have your stockings on?"

The stockings are practically dry already and they make me feel half-dressed. I wrap the towel tighter around my middle and ignore him as I perch on the edge of the wooden bench.

Elias shuts the door and I breathe in the aromatic steam. My trembling wades as if magicked away and I take another deep breath, wishing I was in here alone so I could lie down on the bench and feel the heat seep through my back.

A few moments pass in silence as we both stare at nothing — Elias pouring water on the stones mere inches away, the room filling with steam, my bones finally feeling more human than icicle. I shuffle along the bench trying to make more room but my back is already against the wall.

"We call this *löyly*," Elias says, ladling more water from the rustic bucket onto the glowing stones with focussed precision. His voice is low, almost meditative as the stones hiss in response.

The room immediately grows hotter and my underwear starts to itch. I watch a bead of sweat trickle down the back of Elias' neck and into the fur trim of his Santa jacket.

"You can take your jacket off while you do that," I say. "It's fine, I won't faint from lust."

He ignores me and points to his wooden pail. "That's a *sanko*. We pour the water from the *sanko* onto the *kiuas* and we call it *löyly.*"

"It was Colonel Mustard with the dagger in the drawing room," I mumble, imitating his monotone delivery.

"Huh?"

"Don't tell me that, in addition to *The Flinstones*, you also don't know the board game *Clue.*"

"Do you ever shut up?"

I lean back on the bench, loosening the towel around me as the heat begins to cloud my vision. "Are you used to women shutting up on command?"

He adjusts the hot stones with a stick, sending a cloud of steam into the air. "I'm used to silence and peace."

"Peace! Where? Your village is like a war zone. You can't go anywhere without something trying to kill you."

He turns around, so close the damp velvet of his Santa pants strokes my foot. His gaze travels up my legs, following the full length of my body, up to where I've loosened my towel. Without taking his eyes off me he slowly peels away his Santa jacket, his gaze landing on the top of my stockings which are starting to roll down from the heat. He throws the thick jacket onto the bench beside me, his bare shoulders now appearing to fill half the room. His stomach is taut, his chiseled chest shining with sweat as if sculpted from polished alabaster. He turns back around and I swallow. His back is a maze of corded muscle, flexing and releasing as he labors over the heater.

Damn.

How much wood would a woodsman chop if a woodsman... were this buff? A lot is the answer. He probably chops a lot of wood. Like enough for a small Viking boat...or this cabin. Actually, it's pretty cool to be able to build your own home.

I think of how much wood he would need, which has me thinking about *his* wood, which is a big mistake. Elias is an asshole. I don't care how much birch he's packing, the size of his tree branch is none of my business.

He turns around and stares at me again, his blue eyes flashing with irritation.

"Why are you breathing like a pig in heat?"

Charming. All thoughts of his wood fade as rage blossoms in my chest.

"I'm thinking deep thoughts, Elias. You know how in your head there's just silence and a faint ringing? The rest of us have thoughts swirling up there."

He looks amused. "It didn't look like you were thinking deep thoughts."

Bastard.

I follow the beads of sweat trickling down his hard abdomen and disappearing into the waistband of his Santa pants. Elias catches me looking and I rip my gaze back upwards as he chuckles softly, running his hand through his damp hair.

"You don't know what I'm thinking," I mutter.

"Yes, I do. Because you say it all out loud. You love the sound of your own voice," he says, giving me that irritating smug look of his. "Like all Americans do."

He's still smirking as he puts his Santa jacket back on and opens the door, the cool air like a cold glass of water on a hot summer's day. As he opens it wider I realize he's planning to leave me in here to bake alone, like an insulted piece of cookie dough.

"You're just mad that an American stole your girl," I shout out.

Elias freezes in the doorway, takes a step back, and closes it again.

Shit. I've gone too far. I try to shuffle back but there's nowhere to go, this place is too small. Elias towers over me, his face red from more than the heat of the sauna.

"You don't know what you're talking about."

"I know you have no business running a Santa village. You have the management skills of the guy in charge of the lifeboats on the Titanic."

"You know what? I'm sick of your riddles, metaphors, and ridiculous puns and jokes. Everything you say sounds absurd!" he bellows.

"I'm just saying you're a shit Santa."

He's not. He's actually a great Santa. Watching him with the kids this afternoon was the only time I've seen him truly at peace and happy. But I'm angry and he deserves this.

"And you're a shit reporter," he spits back. "I've not seen you pick up a pen once. Since the day you got here all you've done is complain and eat cookies."

"*I'm* shit at my job? I can't believe you really think you can compete with Christmas World. Have you *seen* that place? I bet their Santa is magnificent." I'm on a roll now and I can't stop myself. "Why do you even bother playing the part? You're not old and you're not jolly, you're totally unconvincing."

"I have no choice."

I roll my eyes. "Oh, I'm sorry. Are you telling me there are no other big, strong men out there who can stick on a beard and be kind to children?"

"No one can be as good as the real thing," he says, his voice quiet and low. "My father is Father Christmas."

OK, now he's completely lost it. Maybe he's permanently concussed from hitting his head on all these wooden beams.

I'm about to make a Christmas version of the *'Luke, I am your father,'* joke but Elias continues talking gibberish.

"My father has been Santa since the very beginning. Our village has been deteriorating for years now and it finally affected his health."

What the hell is he talking about? He sits down next to me, leaning his head against the wooden wall.

"After the costume room went up in flames, my father had a heart attack. It was right before the Christmas season, and he was transferred to a better hospital in Helsinki. That's why he hasn't been around. We couldn't afford a new Santa, and between the cost of repairs and the lack of guests we ended up with no staff. That's why I took over. It was that or we wouldn't survive the season. There's no Santa's Village without Santa, even if he's crap and tired and grumpy and...frightened."

Not one ping. Oh.

He lets out a long breath, and closes his eyes as guilt and shame flood through me. My skin is stinging hot, and not just from the sauna.

I groan inwardly when I think of all the cruel Santa jokes I've made, insinuating his tired mom was his Santa side-piece, and laughing at how stupid he's being for not selling his family business. Now I know what Fjorn meant when he said Elias was in pain. His father had a heart attack, his village is basically Jumanji, and his hot girlfriend left him for a millionaire tycoon who wants to snatch away the last link Elias has left to his family history. And there's me mocking him and doing next to nothing to find out why all of this is happening.

"I'm sorry my investigating has been a little useless," I say quietly, turning to him. He doesn't look at me, instead jumping up and standing by the heater, his back to me.

"You're useless at *everything*," he barks.

"Oh, my God! You don't have to be so goddamned rude all the time!" I shout. Fuck his silence and peace. "You're not the only one going through shit, you know. Your problems don't give you a license to stalk around and ruin everyone's mood."

"Yes, but YOU!" he thunders back, aggressively pouring yet another cup of water onto the stones and swinging around to face me. "You don't need to be so insufferable!"

Elias seems to have doubled in size, every inch of his body occupying the tiny, steamy room. It's like sharing a closet with a bear. Towering over me, I can see the vein throbbing at his temple, sweat gathering at the hollow of his throat, his strong hands gripping the bench beside me, fingers flexing with frustration.

"Me? *I'm* insufferable?" I shout back, standing up on the wooden bench so we're eye-to-eye.

"Yes, you. I'm done with your attitude. Done. I can't take it anymore."

"And what the fuck are you going to do about it?"

We stay like that, his face inches from mine, our angry breaths mingling, his cool blue eyes refusing to leave mine. I want to smack that smug, handsome face of his. He swallows, his soft plump lips parting.

"I'm going to…"

"What?" I say, closing the few inches left between us. "What is this big grumpy budget Santa going to do?"

Elias picks up the pail of water beside him and pours the remnants over my head. I splutter and curse.

"You fucking…"

I don't get to finish my sentence because his lips are suddenly on mine, our teeth clashing together as he kisses me hungrily.

CHAPTER EIGHTEEN

I pull away, panting, his chest heaving in time with mine. He stares at me for an eternity, neither of us wanting to be the first to look away. I want to say something, do something, but I can't move.

His jaw is twitching with anger and for a split moment I think he's going to shout at me again, but then his arm shoots out and in one swift movement he pulls me around the waist and brings me closer to him.

Our second kiss isn't any gentler, although this time it's me raking my fingers through his damp hair, pulling him to me, and deepening our embrace. We crash against the bench, a tangle of lips and teeth, his wet chest slipping against mine and soaking the lace of my bra.

The velvet of his Santa jacket brushes against me, the fur rubbing on the underside of my arms as my hands grasp the back of his neck. I peel the jacket off him and he lifts me from the bench I'm standing on. I wrap my legs around his midsection, the sweat from his torso soaking through my stockings.

Elias whispers my name into the crook of my neck and

my fingernails dig into the back of his shoulders, making him groan. He presses his lips to the dip of my throat in response, nipping at my neck then opening his mouth wider and sinking his teeth into my collarbone.

Oh sweet lord.

He leans me back against the bench and rolls down my stockings one by one before tossing them aside.

"The problem with you…" I continue.

"Enough talking."

He pushes me back over the wooden slats until my head thuds lightly against the bench above me, before sinking to his knees and parting my thighs. I swallow, my fingers tangling in his wet hair as his lips slowly travel up my body until they reach my underwear, his tongue probing against the fabric.

He looks up at me and I smile, biting down on my lower lip. Then he yanks down my panties and throws them beside my ruined stockings, before pulling my knees apart roughly and plunging his mouth between them.

I cry out with pleasure as he works my core with his tongue, arching towards him and pushing him harder into me. All the insults and jokes die on my lips as I feel him travel deeper inside of me, his thumb and tongue working in unison.

I grab his hair and pull him up to meet my mouth, tasting myself on his lips before we break away from one another, chests heaving, words struggling to break free. It's so hot in here that my head is swimming, but the look Elias is giving me has me rooted to the spot.

"I've wanted you, I've wanted this, since I saw you wearing those ridiculous stripy stockings. Even before that…"

He pulls me onto his lap, one leg on either side of him, and deftly unhooks my bra so I'm totally naked. The fabric of his Santa pants caresses my inner thighs, the hot metal of his belt scorching my stomach. The strain of his bulge presses between my legs where I'm already aching, and I can't help but grind against him. I smile as his head falls back and he lets out a low groan.

"I thought you found me insufferable," I say, moving my hips back and forth, feeling him growing harder against me.

"Insufferable," he repeats softly against my neck. "Ridiculous, rude, crass…" He runs his thumb around my nipple and then squeezes it lightly. "But the worse you get, the more terrible things I want to do to you."

I tug at the belt holding up his stupid trousers, and he lifts us both up so I can free him of them.

"Show me these terrible things," I pant into his ear.

Elias doesn't wait for me to tell him twice. Steadying me on his lap, he wriggles out of the pants, sits back down on the bench and I straddle him. We are both soaked with sweat, our limbs slipping against one another, as I slide, inch by inch, onto him.

Elias lets out a deep, guttural growl as I take all of him in and slowly move up and down. My fingers dig into the wooden bench behind him, and I practically leave scratch marks as his lips close over my nipples, sucking hard, clamping onto my behind, and quickening his pace with each one of my cries.

Every inch of us is wet. By the heat of the sauna, the water he poured on me, his sweat mixing with mine, my arousal, our arms and legs and tongue slipping and sliding over one another.

His eyes, heavy-lidded, remain fixed on mine, and I lick at the single bead of sweat trickling down his temple.

His mouth lands on mine and he pushes harder. Faster. More urgent. Using my thigh muscles I grind down on his hardness.

"Saskia," he says, the sound of his name against my skin making me claw at his back. "You drive me mad."

I sit up higher and push down roughly against him as he gathers my hair into his fist and pulls me back, his teeth clawing at my exposed throat before taking my breast into his mouth, his tongue swirling around my nipple hard and fast.

I feel my climax building but I stave it off. I'm starting to feel lightheaded, and it's from more than just the sex. I pull his head back and refocus on his eyes, clasping his jaw as I kiss him and he groans into my mouth.

"It's too hot in here," I moan, running my tongue along his neck. "I'm not built for this."

In one fell swoop he scoops me up and opens the door. "Living room."

The drop in temperature is like a bucket of cold water and my nipples harden instantly. I groan in delight now that I can breathe, shivering as Elias lays me down on the plush rug by the fire beside a stack of blankets.

"Better?" he says, lying beside me.

I inch closer to him and his mouth crashes against mine, my fingers tracing his stomach before caressing his firm ass and pulling him closer

"I like you better in your Santa costume," I say.

"Yeah?" He laughs lightly. "So, tell me…are you on the naughty or nice list?"

"Naughty," I say, reaching between his legs. "Definitely naughty."

He spins me around until I'm on all fours, and I stretch back against him cat-like.

He leans over, pressing his chest against my back, and pulls my face to the side until his lips meet mine. Slowly, his hand snakes around my waist and buries itself between my legs. I whimper softly as he strokes me, fast and rough, his fingers slipping over me, the sweat from the sauna tingling as it dries on my skin. As he kisses me I can taste the salt on his lips.

"Please," I beg, feeling him between my legs. I push back, hungry to feel him inside me, but he edges away. Waiting. Enjoying the tease. I focus on his fingers moving faster and faster. I'm so close. With his other hand he brushes my breast, circling my nipple with the tips of his fingers, mirroring the movements between my legs. But all I can think about is his hardness brushing against my aching core.

He bends forward, sweaty torso meeting my back, and pulls back my hair.

"What do you want?"

I look back him. He's biting his lip, his fingers moving slower now, keeping me on the edge of the precipice.

There's only one thing I want right now. Only one thing I need. I push my head back, his breath on my neck and his ear by my mouth.

"Make me cum, Santa."

With a low growl, he slides hard inside of me and I cry out as he thrusts harder and harder, grasping my waist, pushing me onto him, my whole body trembling as I climax violently. Every nerve in my body pulsates as I squeeze my legs together and grip him tighter.

He keeps pounding me as I thrash beneath him, moving in and out in time to the waves crashing through me. He pulls me back by my hair and finds my mouth, kissing me hungrily, his groans mixing with mine.

I lean forward, my fingers grasping the rug, and look back at him. The fire is reflected in his cool eyes, and our eyes locking makes him quicken. He gets faster, harder, my knees buckling against the plush carpet. I throw back my head and he lets out a roar, his fingers digging into my waist with every last thrust, and we both collapse on the rug.

"Didn't know you had that in you," I say, struggling to speak.

His fingers stroke my back, his breathing in time with mine.

"I have to say," I continue. "I didn't think the Santa outfit and sauna would do it for me, but hey, you learn something new every day."

"Shut up, Saskia," he groans, rolling me over and kissing me again.

CHAPTER NINETEEN

I'm sitting on Elias' living room couch wrapped in one of his woolen jumpers and a pair of his thick socks; nothing else.

I tuck my knees into the jumper and snuggle down against a mound of blankets as he hands me a large steaming bowl of something.

"More reindeer?" I ask with a grin.

He smiles back. "Just vegetables."

He joins me on the couch with his lunch. He looks like a different man. Maybe it's the firelight, maybe it's the sex, or maybe it's this rare moment of quiet.

We haven't had much sleep. The sun has already started to set, even though it's only early afternoon, and the last guest has just checked out of the village so Elias has decided to shut up shop — even though it's Christmas Eve. I'm not complaining.

"It's good you're here," he says, kissing me lightly on the lips. "This is the first time we haven't had guests over Christmas. I'm glad you've been here to help."

Help. I was supposed to help him, yet all I've done is insult him, fuck him and eat his cookies. Another wave of guilt washes over me. To make things worse Elias has been so honest with me, so vulnerable about his dad, and all this time I've been lying to him about who I am. *What* I am.

"I'm not a journalist for *Travel Daily*," I blurt out.

He tears at a piece of sourdough bread with his teeth, chews it, and gives me a steady look. I'm holding my breath. Come on, come on, say something.

"I know."

"What?"

"I know. You're a reporter for a publication on the Blood Web."

My heart quickens. How does he know about the Blood Web? His best friend is a Shifter, but Fjorn doesn't look like he could tell a modem from a microwave. But then the Shifter must know about the Blood Web because he's the one who contacted Jackson.

Oh shit, does Elias know I'm a Witch? My hands are clammy and I suddenly feel very hot. I untangle myself from his side.

"How much did Fjorn tell you?"

He shrugs, bringing his bowl of soup to his mouth and taking a large slurp.

"Fjorn tells me everything. But I could tell you weren't entirely human as soon as I met you."

No *pings*. How did he know? What about me is…inhuman?

"And you didn't care? You didn't wonder what I was?"

Elias makes a noise that sounds something like 'meh' and puts down his empty bowl before pulling me closer.

"When you live out here, surrounded by so much magic, you stop trying to make sense of everything."

Well, damn.

He takes a deep breath. "My ex was…"

"A Witch."

"I was going to say 'different' but... Well, that makes sense. She *was* able to wipe away my headaches with a cup of tea. And you?"

"Same. Well, kinda. I'm a Verity Witch."

"So many Witches," he mumbles to himself.

"I'm not, like, a *powerful* one. I don't do any healing or magic. Well, except for the fact that I can speak every language in the world and can tell the truth from a lie."

"That must be useful," he says, matter of factly, before planting a kiss on the crown of my head.

Silence.

That's it? That's all he's going to say about that? He kisses me again, this time on the lips long and slow, and I melt into his touch.

I guess it is.

"I'm sorry I lied to you," I say.

"Watching you pretend was fun."

"Oh, fun?" I say, sitting astride him, my legs on either side of his strong thighs. "I wasn't sure you were a big fan of *fun*."

He pushes me back on the couch and positions himself between my knees.

"I can have fun."

He pulls up my jumper, revealing my thighs, my hips, and my stomach that's tensing with anticipation. I'm not wearing anything underneath.

"We have very long, dark winters here in Finland," he says, parting my legs and kneeling between them. "I've got very good at making my own fun."

I grasp the back of his head as he works his way down my body. The fire is crackling in the hearth, warming one side of my body, the weak winter sun setting through the frosted windows. I groan as Elias' hand works its way between my legs, then something catches my eye.

A shadow at the window. A shadow, watching us, something small with big floppy ears.

"Errr, Elias…"

"Yes."

He stops what he's doing and I look at the window again. My imagination must be working overtime out here. Just a trick of the light.

"Nothing. Keep going." I close my eyes and give in to Elias' touch. "Don't stop."

The day has passed in a blur of tousled sheets and naps wrapped in Elias' arms. I know this is a winter fling. I know our fleeting relationship is destined to not outlive this year's dismantling of the Rockefeller ice rink, but for now, it's exactly what the two of us need.

It's pitch dark outside and I have no idea what time it is. It's nearly always dark here — it could be four in the afternoon or midnight. Elias doesn't seem to care either way. We're sitting on a bench in his garden bundled in layers of clothing with blankets wrapped around us, and he's pointing at the sky.

"You know Earth isn't the only planet that gets light shows like our aurora borealis," he says. "Jupiter and Saturn have strong magnetic fields too."

Waves of green and turquoise move across the sky. As Elias goes into detail about the collisions of charged particles and talks of Norse gods and Finnish superstitions, all I can think of is Mikayla, who loved astronomy, and my chest aches. I miss her so much.

"My sister would love this," I say, more to myself than anything.

"I bet Christmas is a lot more fun with a sibling. It can be a little lonely being an only child."

"Mikayla is amazing. Exactly what anyone would want in a big sister." A lump forms in my throat and I swallow it down. "But we grew up in Spain, so we never had a white Christmas."

Having a head Witch as a mother also meant we hardly even celebrated Christmas — our community has other end of year celebrations. On warm winter days in Spain, my sister and I would lie on the cool marble floor of our mother's finca and talk about going to Iceland or Finland for Christmas; anywhere cold and snowy and festive.

The only person I've ever mentioned this to is Jackson, once, when I dragged him out for drinks after work for his birthday and I downed one too many Jack Daniels. I'd like to think he's forgotten it all. It's kinda morose.

"Christmas isn't Christmas without snow," Elias says.

I clutch my creamy cup of cocoa with both hands and smile up at him. His face is lit up from the neon sky and pure enthusiasm, as if he painted it himself.

"It's magical," I say.

"It's my home."

I envy him. Having such a deep sense of home, of a place where you belong. Deeply. Your blood rooted to the ground like the trees.

I don't have a home in that sense, so I get why he'd never want to leave The Crazy Reindeer.

"I met a Mermaid yesterday," I say. "She told me a riddle about who or what is attacking your village."

"What?" he says, absent-mindedly.

"In exchange for jam."

"*What?*"

Elias turns his whole body towards me, to see if I'm being serious, then lets out a low whistle. He's still digesting the

fact there are Mermaids in his land when I start to recite the
riddle she told me.

You cannot see
The help unseen,
A master stays unheard.
Listen closely and you'll find
Their manners mean
His song absurd.
Greatest of all time
Bringer of shiny things
Beneath the ancient stone
For him their filthy song still rings.

"Bringer of shiny things?" Elias repeats. "Like someone
rich?"

"I don't know. I've always sucked at riddles."

"I think my problems are linked to me not wanting to sell
the land. It all started happening when people took an
interest in buying the village."

"Have you had many offers?"

"Yes, but Michael Walker is the only one who has offered
me very serious money." Elias shrugs. "That man wants
everything I have...he even stole my fiancé away from me."

Fiancé? *Fuck.*

"I questioned Walker," I say. "He's a serious douche — but
an innocent one."

"I think whatever attacked us in the forest is the same
thing destroying our home," he says. "Which one of your
people is invisible, or small, or bites."

My people? Oh, he means Paranormals.

"You already know *I* bite." I nudge him in the side. He
rolls his eyes but he's smiling. "Vampires bite but they're
never invisible. Witches can cast invisibility spells or curses

where weird things happen but I don't know of any Witches around here except…"

"Kari. And she would never do that. Hullu Poro was like a second home to her before she left."

"I know."

"So what type of creature could it be?"

"There are dozens of small, vicious, and destructive Paranormal creatures but none fit the bill — and they're just the ones we know of. There are still so many variations in hidden corners of the world that are still being discovered, there's no way to tell…" A thought strikes me. "We need to go back to the forest," I cry out. "We need to catch one."

Elias makes a face. "And get attacked again?"

"If that's the only way to follow these fuckers and discover what they are. You've set traps before, right?"

"So you're just assuming I hunt? What, since I'm from Lapland I must know how to set my own traps?"

I think of the deer antlers mounted on his wall. "Well, don't you?"

Elias sighs hard through his nose and puts his arm around me. "Of course I do."

I giggle and nuzzle into him, he smells of pine trees and woodsmoke. Traps can wait.

"Go on then, tell me again, what makes the sky shine like this?" I ask.

"Electrically charged solar particles."

"So your cabins have no electricity but your sky has enough to do *that*?"

He laughs. "The green light is caused by electrical particles passing through the Earth's magnetic atmosphere. You know how a compass points north because of the magnetic pull? Well, that's why we get to experience this magic in the north."

I stare up in wonder, feeling like it would take a lifetime to soak this in.

"Hey," he says, stroking my cheek where a single tear has rolled down. "It makes a lot of people emotional."

"It's not that." I take a shaky breath. "I just miss my sister. She loved all of this."

He doesn't try to console me or come up with a solution, he just holds me tighter as we stare up at the colorful spectacle, taking in both the infinity of grief and the sky. And that's how we stay, both of us lost in our own thoughts until a thundering of hooves breaks the blissful silence.

"I didn't know you'd invited Fjorn," I say, recognizing the reindeer charging toward us.

"I didn't."

Elias is on his feet before I have a chance to flinch at the sudden shape of the Shifter morphing into his naked form. He's out of breath, waving his hands frantically and pointing behind him.

"It's gone," he cries.

Elias is jogging over to him. "What's gone?"

Fjorn is struggling to breathe, sweat dripping down his cold, puckered skin.

"The toy workshop," he says. "It's on fire."

CHAPTER TWENTY

"Are you sure this is the quickest way of getting to the workshop?" I cry, as Elias and I race through the snow on the sleigh, with Fjorn at the front in his reindeer form doing all the hard work. There was no time to hook up the Huskies, and Fjorn was adamant that he'd get us there faster.

"Snowmobile is broken," Elias shouts over the reindeer's thundering hooves. I didn't even know he had one.

The landscape is painted in shades of turquoise and green as the sky continues to swirl above us, every snow-ladened tree bathed in an eerie light. The moon has risen high now, full and bright like a sun. It feels like we're racing towards a magical vortex, a portal into another world.

I reach behind me and take Elias' hand. This is it. This is our chance of catching whatever the hell keeps fucking with his business. I just wish I was armed with more than a sleigh, a shovel, and a bright red bucket.

There's a glow in the distance, far too bright to be anything but fire. The wooden workshop is ablaze, the bright sky muted by smoke. As we get nearer I can see the windows have been smashed and the roof is already sagging from the blaze. The fire is so bright it's turned the green night into day, making it clear to see there are no sleighs or cars nearby.

"Thank god no one was working today," Elias says, reading my mind.

I think back to those three lovely old toy makers and how their livelihood has been ruined — just like Elias' has.

"Firefighters!" I shout as we stop outside the roaring building. Instinctively, I pull my phone out of my pocket only to be met with the usual zero bars. I clamber out of the sleigh while jabbing at the emergency button, surely that still works, but stumble over something making my phone fly out of my hand and disappear into the snow.

"Fuck!"

I grapple for it, my mittened hands going numb from the thick snow, but by the time I find it it's so wet it will no longer turn on.

"Shit. Elias, do you have your phone?"

Fjorn has grabbed one of the furry blankets from the sleigh and wrapped it around his human form. His dark eyes flicker from the lights of the flames. "You're wasting your time. I called the fire department from the village before I found you, but it will take them at least another half hour to get here. We're the only ones who can stop this now."

He tightens the blanket around his waist and races towards the fire, but Elias runs after him, pulling him back.

"There's nothing you can do, Fjorn," he shouts over the roar of the flames.

"But I want to help."

"Then get back to the village and keep an eye on things there. Make sure nothing else ends up in flames. We'll do what we can here before the fire engines arrive."

With a slow nod, Fjorn changes back into a reindeer and speeds off, leaving Elias and me staring at the inferno.

"Here," he says, passing me the red bucket that was hanging off the back of the sleigh. "Get scooping."

While I throw buckets of snow over the flames, Elias does what he can using a shovel. He's working fast but it's like pissing into a volcano. Never have I wished more for better powers. If I were an Elemental Witch, a swipe of my hand could turn a snowdrift into a tsunami and the fire would be out in a second.

I manage to put out a small blaze at the door of the cabin, but inside I can see the workshop has been reduced to a cinder, wooden marionettes singed and swinging like hanged men from the mezzanine floor, small fires erupting just as quickly as we're able to put them out.

"I think there's something inside starting more fires!" I shout out.

Something brushes past my legs and I jump, stumbling over a burned log at my feet. I fall but Elias catches me before I hit the ground, dropping the shovel and kicking the log out of the way.

"Are you OK?" he asks.

I go to answer but someone giggles.

"Did you hear that?"

Elias swings around in a full circle.

"My shovel has gone," he growls.

So has my bucket.

"Show yourselves, you little fuckers," I scream. Not exactly helpful, but this is ridiculous. At least when I've fought supernatural beings in the past I've been able to see what I'm working with!

A high-pitched laugh rings out again and something claws at my leg. I kick out but the force pulls me to the ground. I struggle as Elias grabs my waist, and lifts me into his arms.

"What are they?" he cries.

A pointless question. His eyes dart helplessly to the burning toy shop — his pride and joy. I'm shaking but it's more than fright, and more than cold, I'm so angry. This isn't fair.

"This is awful, Elias," I say, burrowing my face into his neck.

I look up at him. His stubbly jaw is set tight, his watery gaze fixed on the burning flames beside us. He tries to pull away but I hold on to him tighter.

I move us away from the flames that have climbed even higher now. Elias' face is pink on one side from the scorching heat, black smudges mark his pale skin like war paint.

A loud bang rocks the ground beneath our feet and I hold on to Elias tighter. I think of the gas stove inside that Johanna used to make me tea on and try to pull Elias away, but I'm too late. A second explosion causes one of the remaining windows to shatter with such force we are thrown backward. We land in a large pile of snow, Elias' arms protecting me from the fall.

Pieces of splintered wood and charred paper fly through the air around us. I can no longer see the aurora borealis, the smoke making everything around us thick and gray, my nostrils filling with the acrid tang of burning wood and chemicals. The workshop is full of more than just wood; there's paint, varnish, and fabric too. Everything is highly flammable and highly toxic.

The ground is now littered with debris. Elias picks up a small figurine of a wooden reindeer next to my head and studies it. The red and white paint has bubbled and peeled, one leg reduced to nothing but ash. He puts it in his pocket as we get to our feet.

"Ow!" he cries, flinching and jumping back.

Someone laughs a high-pitched cackle. Elias turns to where the sound came from and I feel a pinch at my ankle.

"Ouch!" I shout out.

A victorian orphan-like giggle carries on the air and the faintest of whispers that sound like *you dumb whore*. That can't be right. I'm hallucinating. Surely I'm not being attacked by tiny foul-mouthed ghosts.

"Enough is enough," Elias spits through gritted teeth, marching towards the building.

I chase after him, trying to hold him back from getting any closer to the inferno, but he pushes me away.

"Let me go, Saskia."

Like fuck I will.

I follow Elias into the burning building, the heat stinging my eyes and making them water. I don't even know what we're looking for. The ground is covered with chunks of smoldering debris; damaged toys, singed fabric, and broken tools. The flames have moved from the inside of the building to the roof now, which is raining black dust over us like demonic snow. The timbers creak overhead.

"We don't have much time!" I cry out.

A shadow darts past us and Elias runs further into the building.

"Did you see that?" he shouts, pointing at the corner of the room.

There's nothing there now, just smoke and fresh flames tapering up to the ceiling.

"We have to get out of here," I shout. "We can't save it. The roof is about to collapse."

"But something is in here. We have to catch it."

I cough. My throat is tight with the heat and smoke. Whatever is causing all this chaos is in here, with us, right now - and I very much doubt it's a ghost. Whatever the hell it is, Elias is right, we can't walk away now.

Inside the workshop, he's studying the ground near the painting station. Dark marks like sooty footprints have appeared over the floor and wooden work benches.

"Children?" he says under his breath.

One thing is for sure, curses don't leave footprints. Are these ghosts of children? Child Paranormals? Each option is creepier than the next. I don't have time to analyze every variable, I can't even breathe properly in here. A fit of coughing overtakes me and I look around me for Elias.

He's a few steps away, erratically filling a burlap sack with as many undamaged dolls and figurines as he can find.

"We have to save the toys!" he shouts.

The content of his sack clatters and rings as more toy soldiers, puppets, bells, and little wooden horses are thrown in. Elias moves deeper into the workshop in his quest to salvage all he can, with me running behind him.

"We don't have time for this!" I shout at him as the ceiling creaks above us, chunks of burned wood falling at our feet.

With a glance at the roof, he nods and picks up one last bell from the ground. It chimes in his hand as we run towards the exit. A sound that's a cross between a squeak and a scream rings out from near our feet, but I can't see where it's coming from.

It's dark inside the workshop save for the flames casting eerie long shadows on the wall. Where's the door? Why can't I see the bright white snow or green sky outside?

Elias is behind me.

"There's no way out," he cries out, pointing at a wall. Except it's not a wall, it's the front door that's been blocked by a towering stack of paint cans.

We're trapped.

CHAPTER TWENTY-ONE

Our exit is blocked, and in front of the makeshift wall is a pile of burned wood, broken benches, and what's left of the damaged toys.

"I don't understand. We just came in that way!" I shout out over the crackle of the flames. It's getting unbearably hot in here, and without the air from outside the workshop is starting to fill with thick smoke.

Elias starts to move the pile of trash, flakes of cinder flying through the air and smudging his face, hands, and clothes. The ceiling creaks again and I push him out of the way as a large piece of charred beam falls right where he was standing.

He holds on to me, both of us panting, my fingers digging into his arms. Flames that were on the other side of the workshop are edging nearer, I can feel the searing heat against my back.

"It's not working," he cries. "I keep moving these things out of the way but the pile isn't getting any smaller. I don't understand."

I kick at the debris, trying to reach the pots of paint

blocking our escape, but the smoke is getting too thick and I bend over double, hacking and coughing.

Elias hands me something. It's his scarf, wet from the snow. I hold it over my mouth and instead of moving the wood, I climb over it until I reach the pots of paint. I push at them and one of the tins falls into the snow on the other side.

A gush of biting cold wind hits my face and I drink it in.

"Up here," I shout over the splintering sound of burning wood. The fire has nearly reached us and Elias slips and stumbles as I hold out my hand and help pull him up over the burned pile. Balancing at the top we push through the blocked exit and tumble into the snow on the other side.

Pots of paint topple around us and Elias rolls me to the side as one nearly falls on my head. Snow is in my face and hair, falling into my eyes.

I sit astride him and take a shaky breath, shivering from the cold and the shock, and the adrenaline.

"Are you OK?" he asks, rubbing the tops of my arms.

I nod and stroke his face where a bruise is forming above his eye.

"You?"

His gaze falls over my shoulder but I don't need to turn around to imagine the scene he's watching — the expression on his face tells me all I need to know.

A tin of paint beside us has lost its lid, bright pink paint oozing into the snow. We get to our feet and I lift it as a flicker of light and shadow catches my eye, followed by a high-pitched squeal of delight.

"Over there!" Elias shouts, pointing at another mound of snow.

I can't see anything, yet without thinking I throw the paint in my hand in the direction of the laughter. It splashes against the snow and a squat form immediately materializes beneath the paint. It's furry, with human-looking feet and hands, but large floppy ears like Gizmo from *Gremlins*. Whatever it is, it's no higher than my knee.

"Stinky bitch!" it yells at me, before giggling and running off at warp speed. I run after it, following the trail of pink paint splatters, Elias at my heel.

"Saskia!" he cries. "Stop. Where are you going?"

"To get some fucking answers."

We stumble and trip as invisible forces push against our feet and squeal in spine-tingling glee. We dart among the trees where I can see flashes of pink as the strange fluffy creature tries to escape us.

Icy air fills my aching lungs, my legs burning from running what feels like miles. I look back and realize we're halfway between the workshop and the village. Behind us, in the far distance, I can see the blue lights of an emergency vehicle, and ahead is the warm glow of The Crazy Reindeer village.

The landscape has changed from snowy fields to birch trees, and now we're facing the craggy foot of a large rocky hill. Elias has slowed down and is pointing at something in the distance.

The thing is fluffy, like a cross between a rabbit and a mini sheep. If mini sheep walked on two legs.

This one isn't covered in paint though and I don't think it's seen us. It just stands there, transfixed by the flames in the distance. It's hard to pick out its features in the green hazy light of the night, its white form against the white snow making the creature practically invisible.

I don't recognize it from Blood Web searches, or anything I've ever read about on The Chronicle.

"What the fuck is that thing?" Elias whispers.

"I'm not entirely sure. Why don't we ask it and find out?"

The creature turns to us with a start and then gives us a

slow smile, its beady black eyes shining like lumps of coal in a snowman and thin lips parting to reveal pin-like teeth.

"We need to be careful," Elias says.

Really? *Now* he's deciding to be cautious?

He points at the craggy rock face. "My parents used to warn me about this place as a child."

"But isn't this your land?"

He shrugs. "Well, yes, a lot of this is my land but that doesn't mean I use it all. Some parts of nature you just don't touch."

I look at him, at the strange fluffy thing that still hasn't moved, then at a very normal-looking rock.

"It's just a rock," I say.

Elias shakes his head. "Bad things happen here. Livestock has gone missing and then found dead, right here. Tourists have had nasty accidents. There are strange sounds at night."

"But you said Johanna's stories were all superstition," I hiss.

"It's hardly superstition when it's standing right in front of you," he replies, not taking his eyes off the fluffy creature.

Then Elias blinks. I blink. And the creature disappears. He literally fades away like mist, leaving in its place nothing but a snowy trail leading to a crack in the rock.

Elias takes my hand and we race after the creature. We've only taken three strides when Elias' hand is wrenched from mine and he disappears into the snow. Before I have a chance to work out where he's gone the ground gives way beneath me too and we both plummet through a hole in the ground.

It's pitch dark and all I can sense is the smell of dry earth and something old and rotten. We keep sliding down, the tunnel twisting and turning, as my fingernails grasp at the walls studded with roots and tiny shiny objects.

I can hear Elias shouting below me as I slide behind him, the shoot twisting and turning as we gather speed. Giggles and squeals ring out all around us and then we land, with a huge thud, into the center of a giant cave.

"Are you hurt?" I ask him, clambering off his back.

He grunts an OK and I help him to his feet.

I dust myself off, thankful I was wearing so many items of clothing that padded my fall and look around. It's pitch dark, save for the odd shaft of dull light coming from cracks in the wall.

Then my skin prickles with fear, as somewhere, in the depths of the cave's darkness a choir starts to sing.

CHAPTER TWENTY-TWO

At first, the song is gentle, rising like an angelic chorus of talented children. The notes are heavenly, the voices perfectly matched into a single glorious high note. But the words bring my heart to a skittering stop.

Have yourself a deadly little Christmas,
Fill your heart with fright
Let the winter darkness rob you of your sight

Where is the sound coming from? A shaft of pale light illuminates a corner of the cave and I see a white ball rolling, no...scuttling...past.

As my eyes adjust to the gloom I see another, then another, until dozens of fluffy white creatures scatter like cockroaches along the walls of the cave and wet floor. A few of them run up to us with their long tongues hanging out of their mouths like pink slugs. They bare their needle teeth at me and snicker. These are the creatures we followed, every one of them no taller than my knee, like a bunch of bleached Gremlins.

Elias flinches, looking around for an escape, but there's nothing but craggy walls.

In the semi-darkness, I squint up at the cave's high ceiling where strange clusters are hanging from different heights.

There's a ball of something by my feet, a mass of...shimmering trinkets?

What the fuck?

They must have fallen from the bigger bundle. I grapple on the ground and take a closer look. They're Christmas baubles, some speckled with age and grime, plus tree decorations like the straw reindeer Elias was hanging up the other day. Holding the ball of objects in place above my head is a rope of braided tinsel, now dull and bald with age, with dried holly and Christmas tree lights wrapped around it, none of them lit.

I don't understand.

Attached to the cave's ceiling are clumpy shadows of things swinging eerily as a cold wind blows through the craggy tunnels. Stalactites? No, more Christmas decorations, jumbled and tied nonsensically.

"Hey!" I shout, as out of nowhere a group of white hairy creatures begins to tug at my coat, pulling at the shiny buttons.

I try to shrug them off but they are holding something; a spool of lit Christmas lights. In a dervish of fur and giggles they whizz around me until I'm suddenly bound by a string of colorful lights, my arms pinned to my waist. The creatures push me to the ground and I'm thrown against the wall beside Elias who has suffered the same fate.

"Get off me," he says. His voice is stern and angry, but I can see the flash of anxiety in his eyes. "What are these things?"

The wooly little monsters continue singing. It's like a church service from *Nightmare Before Christmas*.

> *Have yourself a bloody little Christmas,*
> *Kill enemies with spite*
> *String them up and fly them like a fucking kite!*

Another one of these strange Hobbit things materializes next to me and pokes me hard in the abdomen.

"*Fat loser!*" he cries out.

What the hell is wrong with these creatures? Why are they cursing? Why are they singing?

A shattering sound echoes around us and Elias struggles against his binds.

"Don't worry, Saskia. We're going to get out of here," he says, trying to keep me steady.

Then, with a Technicolor flash, the Christmas lights above us start to turn on one by one and I immediately wish we were once again plunged into darkness.

As the lights flash, like some haunted frenzied disco party, they unveil a cave full to the brim with mismatched Christmas decorations and glittering brick-a-brac. It's like Christmas with the hoarders.

Every inch of the ceiling is strung with foil garlands and tree decorations ranging from eighteenth-century ceramic to modern plastic crap – most of which is broken or black with age. Every piece of rock is studded with baubles and tinsel, and a collection of dying Christmas trees lean against another wall, their skeletal branches festooned with even more decorations.

There's only one type of creature who thieves this much and loves to cause trouble.

"Goblins," I breathe.

It's so obvious now!

Elias' shoulder pushes against mine.

"What?" he whispers.

"Goblins. A destructive Paranormal. Small but vicious. And rare."

Very rare. And not invisible, hence why I didn't think of them. As a nearby creature scuttles past an arrangement of decaying gingerbread houses, he momentarily shines and blends with the silver sheen of a bauble installation behind him.

Fuck!

I've read about Goblins being able to camouflage, but I never anticipated that camouflaging in terrain as uni-toned as snow would render someone completely invisible.

"Goblins?" Elias says again. "But...they just look like tiny fluffy sheep."

"They're not common," I say, keeping my voice as low as possible while the creatures busy themselves with counting chocolate coins, rearranging them haphazardly and clutching them to their chest like they're the crown jewels. "I've never seen one before, not even on the Blood Web. Some Paras say Goblins are extinct because they're so hard to find."

"Do they kill?" he asks.

"No. Well, not humans. I don't... I'm not sure."

Elias' face blanches and I feel as sick as he clearly feels.

Goblins don't have many weaknesses. If I remember rightly one of them is sunlight and the other is... *Shit!* Jackson would know. But if I think I'm going to get service in a cave in Lapland then I'm as demented as these critters.

I struggle against the binds of the twinkling, flashing lights wrapped tight around my torso. Tinsel tickles my nose and I sneeze, making the Goblins squeal and run rings around me, sticking even more tinsel up my nostrils.

Elias gasps, his eyes widening. "So *they're* the ones destroying Hullu Poro? But...why?"

I've no idea, but I don't have time to answer as the Goblins have resumed their song.

Clutching Christmas decorations in both hands, carrying them from one side of the room to the other, they move like ants taking leaves to their nests.

"Hey, that's mine!" Elias shouts out as a Goblin runs past with some straw decorations I recognize hanging from his ears like earrings.

The tune sounds like Jingle Bells...but it's not.

Shiny Things! Shiny things!
Rip the angel's wings
Break the bauble
Toil and trouble
Mister Juppi sings!

Who's Mister Juppi?

One by one the creatures line up before us as if preparing for some grand reveal. In the distance, I hear the eerie echo of their song bouncing from the cave's other hidden hollows. Then suddenly, from behind a glistening stalagmite, a tall, angular silhouette emerges from the shadows. Arms and legs jutting out at sharp angles as he tap-dances towards us, beating the ground with his birch staff painted like a candy cane.

What in the fucking River Dance is this bullshit?

The silhouette jumps up on an elevated part of the cave floor and throws his arms wide.

"Allow me to introduce myself." His deep baritone voice cuts the silence of the cave in half, a spotlight hits his face, and my heart drops into my stomach. The creature has the face of a goat, thick curving horns and thin black lips parted in a delighted smile.

"Allow me to introduce myself," he repeats with dramatic

flare. "I am…the Joulupukki."

CHAPTER TWENTY-THREE

"Japalukki?" I say stupidly. The goat man hisses at me. "Jabberwocky?" I try again.

Elias elbows me in the side. I probably shouldn't be trolling the troll, or whatever family of Paranormal crazies this giant half-goat man belongs to.

"THE JOULUPUKKI!" the hideous creature bellows, planting his candy cane into the ground with rage. I put my hands up in defeat.

There's a scurry of Goblins as a group of them come running towards us holding two chairs aloft. As they get nearer I see they aren't holding chairs but gilded thrones, the shiny paint worn thin long ago. They lift us and place us on them, turning us around to face the elevated part of the cave as if we're in the royal box of some grand opera. My memory is suddenly unlocked – he's *Juppi*! The mythical monster the taxi driver warned me about on my way to The Crazy Reindeer. The half-goat Christmas monster. The one who eats children. Great.

Elias and I try to fight back but it's impossible, we are too tightly bound. A Goblin pinches me hard.

'Sit! Watch! Our master is singing!'

Jesus.

A swooping silence blankets the cave as the Goblins all sit down like eager children at a puppet show. They stare up with admiration as the Juppi launches into his solo.

> They say...G.O.A.T stands for
> The Greatest Of All Time.
> And who am I to disagree?
> I'm older than the Christmas tree
> A thousand years old, but still mighty fine
> aging like exquisite glühwein

OK. Let's add narcissism to the list of things wrong with this goat-man.

Elias has stopped struggling, he's watching, mouth agape in sheer horror. I think as far as Elias is concerned, this has gone too far. Reindeer Shifter he could accept. Dating Witches? OK. But a goat monster that sings show tunes? Too far.

This creature is the Paranormal that broke the camel's back.

Juppi clears his throat, and stares me down with his creepy black diagonal irises; aware I'm not fully invested. Then he resumes his song, this time to a gentle hum of acapella from his Goblin minions.

> If I were to deck your halls
> With boughs of holly,
> I might kill you in your sleep
> but your ghost would still be jolly.
> Cause I'm the king of yuletide
> Christmas is my schtick
> As for that other Santa...

This time the Goblins chant in answer as if we're on some messed up Japanese game show.

ST. NICK CAN SUCK OUR DICK!

The Juppi smiles, and I see that his teeth are crusted with blood and...candy cane?

"That's right," he says to the Goblins. "That pesky Father Christmas! I'd eat him if I could."

> *Oh! To be murdered by me...*
> *The greatest Christmas miracle*
> *There's no doubt about it*
> *I am yuletide's pinnacle.*
> *I'm the greatest of all time*
> *The Joulupukki*
> *Though some say, for Christmas, I'm too spooky*
> *My Christmases are biblical*
> *BECAUSE I AM THE ORIGINAL!*

What does any of this mean?

This is like the worst acid trip in the history of Christmas. It's the creepiest thing I've ever seen but I'm not going to lie, I'd give this Juppi guy and his cast a Tony...or three. Hell, the only thing missing from this is Neil Patrick Harris.

Elias hasn't said a word since the goat-man appeared on his makeshift stage, and now he's trying to say something. Words splutter at his lips, then he finally spits them out.

"You can't be real."

That's it? That's Elias' contribution?

"What part of me is not real, my friend?" the goat-man says, jumping off stage, and peering closer at Elias. His face is

159

covered in wiry hair, speckled with crumbs and glitter, spittle collecting along his fleshy lips.

"My fingers?" he wiggles them in Elias' face, making him recoil in horror. "My feet?" He taps out a jaunty little number. "My *teeth*?" The goat man has fangs.

The goat-man has fangs!

"I know…magic…exists here," Elias stutters, doing his best not to look at the monster. "But the Joulupukki, the original scary one, is a myth. A legend. Something parents scare their children with to make them behave before Christmas."

"Oh, yes," the beast bellows, dramatically holding the back of his hand to his forehead. "That's right. I'm the *bad* guy. Listen, you all loved me four hundred years ago when I left gifts for the village children. Back then I was just your everyday goat Shifter, quietly minding my business, but then you humans drove me out of the village and started calling some old bearded *man* your Joulupukki. Rude!"

He twirls his cane again and sings the rest of his song.

I was born a Shifter goat,
Driven out of my home
My craft kept me afloat,
My curse kept me alone.

I straighten up, aware that we're approaching his villain origin story — I need to pay attention. Any second now he will reveal which way he's planning to cook us.

I look around. If only I could find something sharp to cut the ties off these damn tinkling lights!

My mother taught me to sing
My father taught me to whittle
And I've carved pretty things

Ever since I was little.

"Join in now!" he shouts, waving his arms up in the air.

The Goblins scatter, forming into a semi-circle around him, swaying and singing in harmony. Some are holding plastic candles glowing dully in the half-light, and others are swinging broken baubles from their fingers like they're at some kind of Goblin Coachella.

> *He was good, he was sweet*
> *He gave everyone a treat,*
> *Till a Vamp bit him like a cookie*
> *He could no longer shift*
> *And he became...OUR JOULUPUKKI!*

Juppi steps forwards importantly and executes another impressive tap solo. His hooves bang against the ground, as he launches into a final melancholy tune.

> *From that day on I craved blood*
> *And could only venture out at night,*
> *Though still a stud...*
> *My new form gave everyone a fright.*
> *But they say the caged bird sings*
> *So, I kept delivering toys*
> *To all the girls and boys*
> *And in exchange, they would leave me shiny things!*

The Juppi stops and bows to the applause of his Goblins. Their tiny hands clap, sending firecracker sounds exploding through the cave.

I make a face. "You're a *Vampire*?"

Elias gulps loudly beside me. This is crazy. There are

CAEDIS KNIGHT

many Paranormal hybrids out there, but I've never seen an immortal goat Shifter Vamp mix.

Jackson is going to shit himself when I tell him…if I ever make it out of here alive.

The Joulupukki looks crestfallen by my outburst, but only momentarily.

"A Vampire sired me, yes, and that's when it all went wrong because I could no longer shift back into my human form. Destined to stay like this forever — immortal and unchanging — I was unable to deliver Christmas gifts. For hundreds of years, I've hidden away from the light of day in a cave adorned with whatever twinkly Christmas keepsakes my Goblin friends can find me, reduced to nothing but a human goat with sharp teeth and a hunger for blood."

Elias pushes his throne back with his bound feet.

"Oh, calm down, Mr. Lumberjack, I don't drink *human* blood," the goat shouts. "My little fluffy treasures catch me rabbits, or the odd reindeer if I get peckish."

This Juppi-thing is the Goblins' leader and for some reason, they've been destroying Elias' business, yet my chest still aches a little at the crazy Shifter's predicament. His theatrics are clearly a big front for the pain he's been burying for all these centuries.

OK. Whatever. We really need to get out of this place!

These tree lights are wound too tightly around me to fight my way out of the cave, plus I have nowhere to run, but maybe I can talk myself out of this.

"You could still be part of the Para community," I venture. "I'm sure if you explained…"

"Don't be ridiculous! People hate goats, don't you know that? Name one popular goat."

I shrug. "Some people would say Satan is popular."

"Shut up," he snaps. "People don't like goats."

He's clearly based his identity on the fact people don't like goats, I'm not going to argue with him. Not, like, the fact he's creepy as fuck and keeps singing while waving a giant candy cane around!

"Anyway," he says, spinning around slowly. "Christmas is no longer what it used to be."

"That's not entirely true."

"And what do you know of truths?" he mumbles predatorily. "Witch."

CHAPTER TWENTY-FOUR

Well, of course *Mr. Dancing with the Goats* knows I'm a Witch. He must be able to smell my scent like every other Paranormal. Nothing nicer than being the pungent girl at the party.

"No spells," he says, wiggling a bony finger at me. "One magical trick from you and my Goblin friends will eat your boyfriend for dinner."

Elias grunts as a horde of Goblins descend on him, snapping their teeth like fluffy white piranhas.

"Stop!" I shout. "I'm just a Verity Witch. So, actually, the truth is my *only* specialty."

One of the Goblins looks up from Elias' shoes, thick brown laces hanging out of his mouth, then looks back at his master.

"A Verity Witch?" Juppi strokes his goatee beard. "How sublime! I did wonder what all that ringing was when you came in. *Ping*! *Ping*! *Ping*! It's like being in a toy shop at Christmas."

My mouth forms a perfect O.

"You can hear it too?" I've never known of anyone, or any*thing*, being able to hear lies at the same time that I can.

The beast shrugs in an elaborate way. "Goat hearing is exceptional. So is Vampire hearing. How else do you think I can discern what all the little girls and boys want for Christmas? It's also how I retain such wondrous control over my precious little pets." He pats a couple of Goblins on the head and they hum back in response like cats purring. "I thought I could only hear the thoughts of Goblins and children, but it seems your *pings* are also coming through loud and clear. What fun!"

What fun? My already meager abilities have now been reduced to completely useless. We are never getting out of here

I glance at Elias who has the look of a man who has seen so much in such a short space of time he's circled right back to normal.

"You OK?" I mouth at him.

Two Goblins scuttle over to me, one pulls at my hair, while the other pinches my cheeks.

"Ow!" I kick out, and they spit curses at me in turn.

"You're not a Witch!"

"Yeah, where's your broomstick."

"Show us your broomstick. So we can stick it up your ass."

"Ride that broomstick, whore."

"Yeah, Witch bitch."

"Why are your minions so rude?" I cry out at the Joulupukki as one nips my ankle.

He contemplates them, with the half-adoration, half-annoyance of a toddler parent.

"Their vocabulary leaves much to be desired, that is true, but I don't have a lot of choices down here." He gestures wildly at the cave. "For glorious creatures such as myself;

who look like this and can only go out in the dark, the options for forming friendships are limited."

There are about a million-and-one ways Paranormals can find friends on the Blood Web, but I'm not about to start explaining the internet to this ancient monster. Though now I'm curious as to what his dating profile would look like.

"Goblins are foul-mouthed by nature," Juppi continues, picking up a bauble and swinging it back and forth from one claw. "But they love singing and they adore shiny things — so in that, we are aligned."

Another Goblin kicks me and mutters, "*Witch bitch.*"

Juppi may tolerate them but I've had it with these creatures. Another Goblin is staring at me with his tongue out, pretending to masturbate, and I kick out at it.

"Why are we tied up?" I shout out to the crazy Shifter. "What do you want from us?"

He shrugs in an exaggerated theatrical way, then grapevines to the right in time to the music. Why won't these Goblins stop fucking humming?

"The plan was to drive you away. But then you came to me," he croaks. "So I guess I will have to kill you, now."

I feel Elias tense beside me. "Why have you been attacking my village?" he spits, not waiting for an answer. "What have we ever done to you?"

"Nothing. Nothing!" the Joulupukki sing-songs. "But then why does there have to be a reason to be hated, hmmm? Everyone hates me and I was a good little goat. Besides," he shrugs. "It's nothing personal. I'm just following orders."

Elias frowns. "You work for someone else?"

The Joulupukki rolls his devilish eyes and purses his mouth. "Not technically. I simply got an offer I couldn't possibly refuse." He looks Elias up and down, his thin tongue sliding between his black lips. "I'm sure a pretty boy like you knows all about fighting temptation."

The Goblins jump up and down, cackling with glee, as one of them humps Elias' leg. Elias shakes him off, which only makes them laugh and even more of them join in and have a go.

How do I always find myself in these ridiculous situations?

The 'me and a guy I just had sex with trapped in a prison by a creepy monster' look is fast going out of fashion. I clear my throat.

"Tell me who is making you destroy Elias' business," I say. The goat-man's eyes glow a fiery red in the gloomy light, narrowing into distrustful slits. "Please," I add. "Please, your...excellency?"

Flattery is really all I have left.

The Shifter bends down low and whispers something in one of the Goblin's ears, then straightens up.

"Very well," he bellows, throwing his arms out wide. I expect him to launch into another number, but instead he cries out, "fetch me the TEXAN!"

CHAPTER TWENTY-FIVE

id he just say *Texan?* Elias' breaths have turned into little puffs of smoke, each cloud coming quicker and quicker as he puts two and two together. He lets out a strangled growl.

"*Mr. Walker! Mr. Walker!*" the Goblins cry.

There's a flurry of activity as the Goblins get in line and march around the cave, their tiny woolly arms swinging by their side as they start singing a new song.

I strain to pick out the words.

> *Shiny, shiny, things that twinkle*
> *Juppi is our true Kris Kringle*
> *In his cave of gems we thriiiiiive...*

They all stop and face us, like the finale of a Broadway cabaret act, legs kicking slowly from side to side. A can-can of white, sharp-toothed gerbils.

> *And if you're good you'll stay alive!*

With an evil cackle they run out of the cave, chattering about the *'wonderful Mr. Walker'* and *'getting their master some dinner.'*

I turn to Joulupukki, who's leaning against the dripping cave wall inspecting his long talons like he's waiting for a bus.

"What does all this have to do with Christmas World?" I shout at him. "How does Michael Walker know you exist?"

The giant goat stands up straight, his flickering shadow looming over us as he approaches. He puts his face near mine, the Christmas lights wrapped around my arms bathing his matted beard in flashing rainbow hues.

"I get hungry," he states. "And Walker has lots of reindeer. He noticed a few had gone missing last winter and installed security cameras and…voila!" He gives a little tap dance, then taps his candy cane on the rocky floor. "He began to shoot. You know how cowboys love their guns. As fabulous and immortal as I am, no one likes being shot at, not by tranquilizer darts anyway."

I'm not really following, but Elias seems to be.

"Michael is a big game hunter," he mumbles. "Elephants, big cats, and…" He stops as if simply the thought of killing magnificent beasts turns his stomach. "I remember him saying last year how he was going to catch the wolves who were stealing his reindeer. I tried to explain it was more likely wolverines, wolves are rare around her, but he didn't listen."

"I take it Mr. Walker didn't catch any wolves," I say.

"No, no, he caught a lot more than he bargained for." Joulupukki gives a strained laugh, then flaps his hands as if it's all water under the bridge. "But we had a little chat, and I knew Mr. Walker would be a reasonable man. After all, anyone who owns such a big, shiny car and wears that many rhinestones can't be all bad. I explained how difficult life can be for a goat god and his minions, and the Texan and I struck a deal."

"Unlimited meat and a cave full of baubles?" Elias sneers.

"No!" the goat-man roars, his mouth twisting into a vicious snarl. "I just want…"

Before he has a chance to answer one of the Goblins tumbles back into the cave, his eyes wide with confusion and his tiny hands flapping by his side.

"Master! Master! Your dinner has gone bad!"

Four other Goblins are wrestling with something in the shadows, their giggles and squeals mixing with human moans of distress. As they step into the light I can see they're pushing a naked man into the clearing.

"Fjorn!" Elias cries out.

The Goblins are flustered and running around in circles, their little hands pulling at the tufts of hair on their downy heads. Their cackling cries echo through the cave.

"Reindeer supper!"

"We have to feed our Juppi."

"Juppi loves Reindeer tatare."

. *"Reindeer on the bone."*

"But the reindeer turned human!"

"Elias?" Fjorn runs forward but the Goblins group at his feet, making him trip and skim his knee on the rocky ground. In a whirl of pale limbs, Fjorn bats them away, while at the same time trying to cover his modesty. His hair is tousled, tangled with tinsel and holly leaves, and his arms are full of tiny scratches from the Goblins' sharp teeth and nails.

"Let my friends go!" Elias shouts, although we all know he's wasting his energy. The Goblins ignore him and continue their chants.

"Getting angry makes the meat tough."

"Master likes his dinner tender."

"Deep, calm breaths, Rudolph the big butt reindeer."

"I already told you. I'm *not* a reindeer. I'm a *Shifter*," Fjorn cries. "Just like that…Goat Shifter monster thing you all love so much."

Joulupukki has melted back into the shadows, although his red eyes continue to glow in the dark. Watching. Waiting.

A Goblin jumps on the shoulders of another and lunges forward. *"Cover up your micro balls!"* he squeaks, punching poor Fjorn in the modesty.

Fjorn drops to his knees, eyes swimming with tears. Another Goblin smacks him on the back of the head.

"Tiny penis! Missing antlers!"

Christ almighty, it's like Fjorn is being hazed by a bunch of stunted fraternity guys.

"You don't have a small penis, Fjorn," I blurt out.

Out of the corner of my eye, I sense Elias staring at me, but what am I meant to do? This poor guy is having his genitals ridiculed by a bunch of fluffy ankle-biting Goblins.

"Hey!" I cry out at one of the critters. "Stop flicking it."

They giggle raucously as Fjorn shuffles over to the corner, his legs locked together.

"You have a nice penis," I continue, nodding encouragingly. "I've seen quite a few in my time and that one is…" I glance at Elias again and clear my throat. "Ignore them, Fjorn. They're being mean."

A Goblin jumps up like an Olympic athlete and pulls my hair.

"Horny Witch bitch!"

Ow! What the fuck is the matter with these freaks? I can safely say these are my least favorite Paranormals that I've ever had to deal with.

I kick out at the Goblins again as they jump about my feet making more lewd gestures. Elias looks like he's either going to hit someone or vomit. He strains against the flashing strand of lights binding our arms to our sides, but there's no way we are getting out of here by brute force alone.

Fjorn cowers against the wall as the Goblins pinch and prod him.

"Let me go," he says weakly, but they keep him on his knees as if in prayer or reverence. That's when I realize who it is the Goblins expect the reindeer Shifter to be worshipping.

The Joulupukki steps out of the shadows and Fjorn recoils. Then, with inhumane speed and the sound of hooves scraping against stone, the beast is suddenly next to him.

Fjorn keeps his head down as the Joulupukki strokes his thick, tangled hair as if thanking him for his adoration. He runs a dirty hooked claw from Fjorn's shoulder down to his hand, massaging his fingers in his. Then he sings one final word, holding Fjorn's arm up to the light.

"Delicious."

And before Elias or I can do or say anything, the beast sinks his fangs into Fjorn.

CHAPTER TWENTY-SIX

Blood spurts out of Fjorn's wrists, painting the walls of the cave like a gruesome Pollock while the Goblins dance beneath the fountain of blood as if it were rain.

The goat-man's muffled moans of hunger echo through the cave as he feasts on our friend. I'm screaming and Elias is trying to gnaw his way out of his binds, but the Joulupukki doesn't even look up as he slurps and moans into Fjorn's flesh, his beard matted black with blood.

I know enough about Vamps to know that biting to eat and biting to turn are two very different things. Fjorn won't necessarily die as long as the Joulupukki slows down once the reindeer Shifter begins to weaken, except he's showing no signs of stopping. Fjorn slumps onto the ground, resigned, drained as if his bones have been taken out of his body along with his blood. Elias is struggling to free himself as I scream at the beast to stop, when a voice cuts through the Joulupukki's sounds of pleasure.

"Looks like I've arrived at the party just in time!"

Juppi pulls his fangs out of Fjorn's arm and drops him to the ground, dabbing at his mouth daintily.

I focus every morsel of my energy on Fjorn, watching him, looking for a sign of breath.

His fingers twitch and I breathe out, Elias following my gaze, his own shoulders slumping in relief.

Our friend is alive. Barely.

"Ah, the magnanimous Mr. Walker," Juppi cries out, running his thin black tongue over his blood-stained fangs.

Walker is strutting over to the makeshift stage like he's won first prize at the rodeo. He tips his white Stetson at the Joulupukki, the rhinestones on his jacket twinkling in the gloom of the cave, then jabs Fjorn with the tip of his cowboy boot. The Goblins gather around the tycoon, their tiny hands held up like baby birds waiting to be fed.

"Howdy, there, my pretty lil Pixies."

Stupid fucking idiot, getting involved with my world while not even knowing his Pixies from his Goblins. I'm so angry all I can do is let out a low growl as I watch him scattering Swarovski gems to the ground like birdseed, the kind of gems I saw for sale in one of his gaudy Christmas shops. Dozens of Goblins run around excitedly, plucking the crystals from the ground like a flock of hungry chickens.

Walker turns full circle and, upon seeing Elias and I wrapped up in Christmas lights, lets out a laugh like a loud bark.

"Well, what have we here?"

He squints in the darkness, trying to see who we are.

"*Haista vittu!*" Elias spits, telling the Texan to fuck off.

Walker steps closer, his face lit up in colorful flashes from the Christmas lights wrapped around us.

"If it ain't the lowly innkeeper and his bit on the side," he drawls. "You know I have no idea what you are saying, Elias, so sticks and stones and all that. And who's the naked guy on stage? He looks wrung out. My, you Fins have some strange kinky Christmas customs."

Elias is practically frothing at the mouth.

"You piece of shit!" he screams. "What did you promise the goat to make him terrorize my village for the last year? You've ruined my business, my family, and...Christmas!"

Walker laughs. "I've ruined Christmas? What's the matter? You just found out Santa ain't real?" He sweeps his hand out, pointing to Joulupukki and the Goblins. "Me and the gang here came to a special arrangement." He winks at me, and I spit at his smug face, missing him by a mile. "What can I say, sugar tits. I'm a great negotiator."

"You're not from here. You don't understand our traditions or respect our myths and legends," Elias shouts. "You have no place coming here and taking over our land, then threatening the Joulupukki into terrorizing his own community."

"I don't need to be Finnish to finish you off," Walker chuckles. "It's just business, it ain't personal. And I didn't have to threaten the old goat, either, he was more than happy to help me when I offered him what you locals took away from him years ago." He lowers his face closer to Elias, whose own is twisted in pain and anger. "I told you, you should have sold up when I gave you the chance."

Elias leans back, his shoulders sagging in defeat. "Does Kari know about this?"

The Texan laughs. "Ah, my little angel. The less she knows, the better. She loves me for the same reason these little critters do."

The Goblins are now holding hands and dancing in a ring around Walker.

"I give my gal all the pretty shiny things her heart desires. Unlike you, eh? What were *you* able to give her?"

A Goblin bares his teeth at Elias. "*Tiny Tim the lowly loser!*"

Walker scatters more Swarovskis from his pant's pockets and into the air like confetti. "That's right, boys. Who's your daddy?"

God, this man is the absolute *worst*. He makes Juppi look like something from a petting zoo.

While the attention isn't on me, I use the time to try and work out what the hell the goat and Texan's exchange was. So the Goblins are happy with their shiny little trinkets, and Juppi has somehow been convinced to cause havoc in exchange for some kind of retribution, but what I don't get is why Walker is so desperate to get his hands on Elias' Christmas village? Surely getting his girl and all the Christmas Lapland tourism business is enough punishment for poor Elias. Why does he want to hurt him further?

I look around at where we're sitting. The cave is, well, cavernous. Huge. But it's not its size or the ridiculous amount of old Christmas ornaments that catch my eye — it's the way the walls are glowing a pale lilac. Where we entered was wet and slimy, but further along the tunnel that Walker just emerged from it looks drier and...sparkly.

"Do you own the land above this cave?" I whisper to Elias. He nods.

"So your family owns this cave as well?"

He shrugs. "I didn't know it existed but...yes, I suppose we do."

Jackpot!

CHAPTER TWENTY-SEVEN

T here must be something down here that Walker wants. This is beginning to make a lot more sense now. I twitch as the Goblins bustle around us with their new Swarovski loot. Like a hoard of crafters, they scuttle to and fro, clutching their gems, as if deciding what to bedazzle next. But it's not them that I'm worried about now.

The Texan is pressed against the cave wall talking in hushed tones to Juppi, the goat Shifter towering over him and nodding along to whatever he's being told. Frustratingly, I can't hear any of their whispered discussion over the Goblins' excitable jabbering. They're probably deciding which one of us the Joulupukki will feast on next.

I look over at Fjorn. He's managed to crawl closer to us and is still conscious, although his eyes are barely open. Blood pools around his shivering, curled-up body and Elias looks over at me, pleadingly. But there's nothing either of us can do while we're tied up and stuck underground.

OK. I need to focus…if only there were something close by that we could use to cut our twinkling restraints.

I peer deeper into the cave and can just make out a series

of tunnels in the distance. Where shafts of moonlight hit the craggy walls they glow in shades of purple and lilac. The stone is familiar, but I'm struggling to make out the large, dark shapes in the distance.

Then I realize what they are. Tools! Like the old-fashioned pickaxes that the seven dwarves carry in the Snow White cartoon. There are also some battered wooden carts on a rail and part of the wall is held up with beams. It reminds me of a coal mine — not that I've ever been inside a coal mine before. So this is more than just an abandoned cave.

I lean over and whisper to Elias.

"Do the Finnish mine for coal?"

Elias furrows his brow. "Not that I know of. Some gold and nickel are mined in this country, but Lapland is more famous for its amethyst."

Amethyst, of course!

I think back to the Christmas World market and the stalls selling local produce.

What was it Walker said to us? *'Everything sold here is sourced locally.'*

Is this the cave where he's been getting his amethysts from?

"I know what you're after," I shout out to Walker. They both look up at me, unamused that I've interrupted their conversation. "You want Elias' land because you want this cave!"

The Texan brushes invisible dust from his shoulder.

"Hush your mouth, little girl," he says. "The big boys are doing business over here."

Elias leans over to me. "Why would he want this cave?" he whispers. "There's nothing here but a load of Christmas trash."

"And gemstones."

Juppi looks over at us again, his excellent hearing honing in on my words, and cocks his head to one side like a raven.

"This cave is full of amethyst," I say to Juppi. "That's where Walker has been getting the stones to sell in his Santa village and probably further afield."

"Yes, so what?" The goat shrugs. "There are more than enough pretty minerals down here for everyone. Boring, boring. Anyway, my Goblin friends and I prefer Christmas sparkle to dull, old stones."

"Baubles! Baubles! Baubles!" the Goblins chant.

Walker laughs and straightens his Stetson.

"Don't you worry your pretty little head about me and my business. Mr. Goat and I have a deal. We trade in gems and favors. That's no secret."

"And what exactly has he offered you in return?" I ask, giving Juppi a pointed look.

The goat Shifter beams at me, his teeth stained red and speckled with pieces of hair and leaves. I try not to think back to the image of him attacking our reindeer friend.

"This fine gentleman promised me what I've always wanted — the chance to be the Father of Christmas once again. To run my own Christmas village and give gifts to all the boys and girls."

The Texan beams, hands on his hips, looking around him like he's already standing in the middle of his own amethyst palace. There's no way Walker would ever let this beast anywhere near his Christmas World.

"He's lying!" I shout.

The goat makes a face at Walker who chuckles.

"Now, now, missy. Beautiful things are at their prettiest when they stay still and silent."

There has to be a way I can make Juppi see he's being conned. I strain against my binds, which is even harder as the Goblins are now sitting on our laps and the armrests of these ridiculous thrones like we're at the movie theater. Elias gives a long, resigned sigh, accepting that this is his lot now.

I sneeze. There are so many of them it's like being smothered in a thick sheepskin rug. I'm surprised the Texan can hear anything I'm saying with all this fur on my face.

Wait. The goat Shifter can *hear my pings*.

I wriggle until a couple of Goblins fall off me.

"So tell me all about your grand idea," I say pointedly to Mr. Walker. Juppi's face contorts into one of curiosity — my words have strung a chord. Of course, they have. The goat's not stupid, he knows exactly what I'm doing.

"Do you think the grand Joulupukki will make a good Santa in your Christmas village, Mr. Walker?"

The Texan puffs out his chest and beams a big fake grin. "Mr. Juppi will be the perfect finishing touch to Christmas World," he roars, patting the beast on his hairy arm. "I can't wait for him to join us."

A *ping* echoes out, quickly followed by another. The goat frowns, squinting at the Texan, then looks at me.

"I suggest you ask your business partner some pertinent questions," I urge the goat, whose expressions keep flickering from confused to suspicious. The Goblins aren't following this either but they know something is about to go down and start wriggling on my lap with excitement.

Juppi clears his throat. "Mr. Walker, are you saying I would make a bad Father of Christmas?"

Walker shakes his head, his wide Stetson wobbling on his head.

"Quite the reverse. You are clearly a magnanimous, approachable, and fun kinda guy. Now you finally have Elias out of the way I will organize the village for you immediately."

Five consecutive *pings* ring out loud and clear, echoing

through the cavernous tunnels surrounding us. Juppi's face falls, and the Goblins, having detected the change in their master's mood, jump off us and begin to gather around the beast's feet.

"Master! Master! Master!"

Juppi continues with his questions. "Mr. Walker, you said that if we were to scare Elias and his family away from his land so that he'd sell you his village, you would hand it over to me."

Walker swallows and fans himself with his hat, clearly confused as to why Juppi is suddenly so angry.

I wink at Elias and sit back because my work here is done. The goat knows Walker is lying to him and he's about to hand the Texan the shovel to dig himself deeper and deeper. I wish I had some toffee cinnamon popcorn to hand. I wish I could *move my hands*.

"Yes, yes, you will get the village," Walker says. "I just want the cave."

Just one *ping!* this time.

"I may be very old," Juppi says. "But, did you know, like any Vampire Shifter hybrid, I can still be killed? As can my beautiful Goblin friends."

Vampires die a slow death in sunlight and Goblins turn to stone. It wouldn't take much for Walker to trap them all and leave them outside at midday.

"I…I..didn't know that," Walker stutters.

With every *ping!* the goat Shifter's red eyes glow more fiercely.

"What's happening?" Elias whispers, edging his seat closer to mine.

"Your nemesis' downfall," I whisper back. "I may not have many powers, but at least the Christmas goat has great hearing."

Juppi's face is now inches from that of his business partner, who is doing a really bad job of looking calm and collected.

"So you planned to use me and my team to help you get Elias' land, keep my precious cave, then kill us all?" the beast snarls in the Texan's face. "*That* was your plan?"

"No!" *Ping!* "Of course not." *Ping!*

Both Elias and Fjorn are staring over at me wide-eyed, realising exactly what is playing out before us, and all I can do is grin. The Goblins are getting restless, muttering and chattering like nesting birds at our feet.

"*Master is angry.*"

"*Master is sad.*"

"*We must help Master.*"

"You lied to me," Juppi says quietly, dabbing at his devil-like eyes with a frilly handkerchief. Where the fuck did he get that from? "My entire life people have hated me, feared me, they even stopped believing in me...but they have always *respected* me."

He bangs his cane on the ground, the sound echoing all around us. "No one has ever been stupid enough to *lie* to me, Mr. Walker!"

With every word the goat utters the Texan slowly backs away, until with a yelp he turns and runs. His white leather cowboy boots echo off the slimy walls as he slides and stumbles towards a dim spot of light in the distance, but he can't outrun a horde of Goblins.

"I am bereft," the goat howls against the backdrop of dozens of Goblins whooping and squealing as they chase the Texan down the winding tunnels in the distance.

Elias and I edge our seats to the side so we can get a better look at the Texan's silhouette getting smaller and smaller while a sea of white fluff closes in on him.

Michael Walker may be rich, and he may have the glitziest Christmas village in Lapland, but he's not fast. With a sound like Santa's sack being slung into the back of a sleigh, Walker hits the hard ground and the Goblins pin him down.

"Bring him to me," the goat wails, holding the back of his hand against his forehead.

Walker is squealing and cursing as a tidal wave of Goblins drag him back to the makeshift stage, his nails scraping along the cave's grimy wet floor as he attempts but fails to fight back.

The Goblins pull off his hat, one of them sitting on his back waving it around like a rodeo show, two others pull off his boots, and start to sing to the tune of Jingle Bells.

Mr. Juppi, Mr. Juppi
He hates all your lies
Oh, what fun it is to eat
Mr. Walker's eyes.
Mr. Juppi, Mr. Juppi
Suck his bones and teeth
Oh, what fun it is to eat
Mr. Walker's feet!

My God, it's a cannibal's choir — only instead of Chianti and fava beans, Juppi will likely pair Mr. Walker with glühwein and jelly beans.

As the Goblins chant and sing in the Texan's face, ripping at the crystals and buckles from his hat and boots, Fjorn uses the opportunity to shift back into a reindeer and stagger over to us.

He leans into Elias, his fast breaths like warm clouds, his injured arm now a mangled reindeer leg. Another patient for the angel doctor. Thank God Walker arrived when he did or Fjorn would not have lived to tell this tale.

"The lights," I say, glancing at the Goblins to ensure

they're not watching us. They're not, they're line dancing in a ring around the cowboy.

Fjorn bites through the chords and Elias and I rip our binds off us, shaking out our numb hands and feet. My arms feel bruised where the string of lights has been biting into my skin, but other than that we got off lightly.

"Are you OK?" Elias says to me, pulling me close and planting a kiss on the crown of my head.

I don't have time to answer as Fjorn is butting our butts with his muzzle, signaling for us to jump onto his back. He's right, we have to get out of here. I take Elias' hand and clamber on to the reindeer but he's not even taken three weak steps forward before Joulupukki has already spotted us.

"Stop!" he shouts, grabbing Fjorn around the neck and pulling us all down. We tumble to the floor, in a tangle of hooves, arms and legs. Walker is still being pinned to the ground by the Goblins, veering from shouting obscenities to the Goblins, to promising them and their master the world.

"You can't leave now," the goat says to us, his voice like sandpaper on stone. "I'm still a little peckish."

A shiver runs through me as I watch the hunger grow in his eyes, spittle collecting at the corner of his black lips.

We cower on the ground as his nails grow longer and slowly, he rises on his thin, hooved legs, ready to pounce. I bury my face in Fjorn's fur, Elias holding us both tightly.

But it's not us the beast wants.

With a deafening cry, the Joulupukki plucks Walker off the ground like he's nothing but a piece of Christmas trash. Some of the Goblins are still clinging to the Texan tightly and they slide back to the ground with a cackle.

"Please," Walker pleads, his suit bunched in the goat's fists and his raised feet peddling three inches off the ground. "I will give you all I have; my money, my businesses, my girl…"

No *pings* this time. He would sacrifice his *girlfriend*? But the Shifter hybrid doesn't let him finish.

With a sickly crunch, the beast takes a bite out of the Texan's torso. A fountain of blood soaks us all as we watch the goat re-enact Goya's *Saturn Devouring his Son*. The Joulupukki's eyes shine like two crimson harvest moons in the dim light of the cave as he rips at the man's flesh, the Texan fast reduced to nothing more than a bundle of blood-soaked rags and bone.

Elias and Fjorn turn away but I don't. I've seen a lot worse in my line of work.

The Goblins cheer their master on as they skip hand-in-hand around him, the cave ringing out with the sound of their shrill singing accompanied by the crunching and snapping of bones. Pieces of clothing drop to the floor with a squelch as the Joulupukki pulls tufts of hair from his wet mouth.

Silently getting to our shaky feet, Elias, Fjorn, and I back away slowly, but we can't escape the attention of the Goblins who run over and jump onto our legs, holding us back.

Joulupukki looks up, giving us a sticky crimson smile, blood dribbling from his long fangs.

"The Texan is not as flavorsome as venison," he says to Fjorn, spraying us all with blood and gristle as he speaks. "But after a couple of centuries, everything starts to taste like chicken."

"We've done you no harm," I say. "You heard the *pings* of lies and none of them came from us. Please let us go."

The goat Shifter flings something over his shoulder. It may have been a femur or humerus — I'm more of an expert on boners than bones — and looms over us. We shrink back.

"You can't leave," the goat says again, his features growing solemn as he places Walker's mangled remains at our feet like some kind of offering. I swallow down the bile building in my throat.

We're next.

"I should not have trusted that man," the goat cries out, looking around him as if performing some Shakespearean soliloquy. "You and your family didn't deserve the chaos we brought to your lives. I am ashamed." He holds out one sticky hand. "I am beholden to you." He holds out the other, this time flinging Texan gristle over the cave walls.

Wait. *The Joulupukki has a conscience?*

Elias stirs beside me, then steps forward. "I have a proposition," he says.

Really? After everything he's just witnessed, he's going to bargain with the goat? The Goblins are still circling us like tiny white sharks, nipping at our ankles. I'm pretty sure all Goblins are herbivores, but perhaps watching their master feed has made them hanker for some red meat too.

"Elias," I whisper. "We need to get the hell out of here. Don't negotiate with him! This isn't a fucking Christmas market."

"No, no, no, my dear child. Let the handsome man speak. I do love a good bargain," Juppi drawls. He poses his chin on his hoove, in dramatic anticipation. "Do continue."

"Batshit Broadway is going to murder us," I say between gritted teeth.

"Silence in the audience," Juppi snaps at me, then nods at Elias to continue speaking.

"My suggestion," Elias says. "Is that you and the... Goblins...will repair all the damage you have caused in my village, and you will use your..." Elias looks around cave, "...*resources* to ensure Hullu Poro becomes Lapland's most authentic and popular Christmas Village."

The Joulupukki points his finger in Elias' face. "And what do I get in return?" he snaps. I hold my breath as the stench of raw human flesh smacks me straight in the face. "What could you possibly offer that would be a sweeter Christmas treat than peeling your skin away, inch by inch?"

Gross!

Elias smiles mischievously. It's not something he does often, but it suits him.

"How would you like to be Santa?" he says.

CHAPTER TWENTY-EIGHT

It's Christmas Day in Lapland and I'm alive. I was hoping for a Nordstrom gift card in my stocking this year, but 'not dying' is a close second.

I pull the comforter over my shoulders and snuggle up to Elias, his arms closing around me tighter.

"Merry Christmas," he murmurs, planting a kiss on my lips.

We didn't sleep much last night. By the time we convinced Fjorn to head straight to the infirmary, then staggered home, showered so long our skin hurt, and fell into bed it was already some point in the morning. My dreams were full of high-pitched singing and cackling, blood and crunching bones, and judging by Elias' twitching all night I doubt he slept much either.

"Merry Christmas," I whisper back.

I feel him stir beside me and he grins, nuzzling my neck as his hand slips beneath the covers. I groan as he moves up my thigh and gently strokes me, my fingers grasping at his hair, pushing him deeper into the crook of my neck.

Narrowly escaping death is a fantastic aphrodisiac.

Elias' phone rings on the nightstand — the type of old cell phone that I'm sure is in museums now — and he glances at it before snatching it up with urgency and leaving the bed. I frown. So much for my festive fuck.

"Mom! Is everything OK? How is he? You're coming home! Yes, of course! That's wonderful."

He turns to me, his eyes shining with glee.

"My father is better," he says, scrambling out of bed and pulling a thick jumper on. "They're coming home."

"Yes, I heard."

Elias' grin is infectious and I can't help but join him.

"So I guess everything is going to be OK now," I say.

He nods enthusiastically and I follow him downstairs where he adds logs to the fire that has died down overnight.

"I'm almost too scared to hope that things will go back to how they were before Walker…"

He trails off and I rub his arm.

"That man can't hurt you or your business anymore. He's gone."

A shadow passes over Elias' face. I've reminded him of what we saw, the crunch of bones and flesh dropping to the cave floor. I wonder if he's thinking of his ex, Kari. The same doctor whom no doubt helped Fjorn last night and will now never see her lover again. Walker was a terrible human being, but he was still her boyfriend. Does she know he's gone for good?

Elias swoops me into his arms and pulls me close, enveloping me in the warmth of his woolen jumper. The fire crackles and his lips on mine make me want to curl back in bed again.

My stomach rumbles and Elias laughs.

"Food first," he says, pulling me over to the kitchen where he begins to put together an elaborate breakfast of scrambled eggs with smoked salmon, Joulutorttu pastries, and thick oatmeal.

"Try this," he says, passing me a birch mug full of coffee.

"Did you carve this yourself?"

"Of course." He scoops up the Halloumi-type cheese he was just chopping and drops it into my coffee.

"You know they're not sugar lumps, right?" I say.

He gives me a scathing look. "It's called *leipäjuusto*, otherwise known as bread cheese. It's made from cow milk, although sometimes reindeer or…goat. Never mind. Try it. The taste can't possibly be worse than some of your fake American food."

"Hey, watch it, buster. Where I live, we get squirty cheese from a can."

I take a sip of my cheesy coffee, expecting to gag, but it's actually amazing. The scent of the birch mixed with the sharp sour coffee and salty cheese has me asking for seconds in seconds. Elias laughs, shakes his head, and points to something in a bottle.

"Drink this next. My mother made it for Christmas Day breakfast every year," he says, sliding a tall glass of something red over to me. It's cute how much he's enjoying his culinary Show And Tell this morning.

I take a sip from the glass. Strawberry. Oh my god, why isn't strawberry juice a thing anywhere else?

Sitting up at Elias' kitchen table, he keeps serving me dish after delicious dish, which I'm eating faster than he can cook.

"Amazing," I say between mouthfuls of dark bread and salmon, pancakes, waffles, and my favorite — the rice pudding pastries.

Elias finds my enthusiasm very amusing.

"Having a nice day so far?"

I grin and nod, and he comes up behind me and kisses my neck. A long, sensual kiss that has my stomach twisting with desire. He points above him where a huge bunch of mistletoe hangs. It doesn't look real. When did he hang that up?

"Is that plastic?" I say.

"I found some amongst some old decorations. Kissing beneath it is an American custom, right?"

I nod and kiss him again. At this rate, we are going to spend the whole of Christmas Day making out. I stare over his shoulder at the forests in the distance heavy with snow. There's no daylight yet, making it late morning by my guess, or maybe early afternoon. Time works differently this far north.

"My first white Christmas," I say, opening the window and marveling at the thick snow that has settled on the ledge overnight, the latticed windows decorated with frosted lace.

The view at the back of his cabin is endless fields and forests, much prettier than what's left of his shambolic Christmas village. I close my eyes at the thought of how long that is all going to take to get back to normal, not to mention the expense.

We're the only ones left at the resort.

Fjorn left Elias a note under the door to say he'd been healed and that he was heading into the forest to deal with some unfinished business. Something about life being too short. Elias seemed to understand what that meant.

I should stay and help him get things back to normal, but how can I? I have an article to write and a life in New York and an editor that will be breathing down my neck soon.

I wrap my arms around his neck and kiss him. "Want to build a snowman?"

"Such a Disney thing to say."

He laughs, spinning me around and making me yelp. He kisses my collarbone and I instinctively push myself against him, groaning with pleasure. I don't want to go back to reality. I want all this to last longer; the cozy log cabin, snow, a roaring fire, a big burly Fin who can't stop kissing me.

Something hard pushes against my hip. I reach down.

"Is that a log in your pocket or are you just pleased to see me?"

He rolls his eyes and holds something out to me. It's as large as the palm of my hand and looks like a thick piece of lilac glass.

"I got this from the cave last night before we left," he says. "*My* cave. My new amethyst mine. It's my gift to you."

I take it from him and hold it up to the weak light that's beginning to break through the clouds.

"I love it," I breathe.

"It's so you never forget Lapland."

I look up at him and in that moment we both know. This thing between us, it's not forever, it will only ever be a holiday fling. It's been beautiful and special, and absolutely fucking terrifying, but unlike a cute little puppy, this IS just for Christmas. I'm going to miss him, though. All of it.

My phone message alert rings out and I untangle myself from Elia's embrace, running upstairs to the bedroom. My first thought is my sister. We always spend Christmas together. Wherever she is, whatever she's running from, she'll definitely want to talk to me today.

I turn on my phone screen and scroll through...but it's not her. It's a notification from the Blood Web messaging system.

Jackson.

I hope you are having a nice Christmas! Check your bag, I left you something.

I throw my phone on the bed, blinking back tears. Fucking Jackson. He probably sneaked my next assignment in among my thermals.

What joys do I have awaiting me in New York this

winter? A gang of Brew Witches making people's New Year's resolutions come true? Turkey Shifters seeking revenge on meat-eaters after two months of excess?

The faint sound of singing floats up from outside. *Oh no.* Not more festive carols. I drag myself to the window and look outside, but there's nothing but mounds of snow and trees.

The singing gets louder and I run downstairs to the living room where I find Elias with his head out of the window. He slams it shut and turns to me, his eyes wide with fear.

"They're back," he says.

"Who? There's no one there," I reply.

"*Exactly!*"

He's running around the cabin, locking the windows and double bolting the door.

His pale face flickers in shades of orange and yellow from the roaring fire. "What if they changed their minds? What if they've come back to kill us?"

"Hey," I say, squeezing his hand. "You made Juppi a promise, and you meant it. He could hear there were no *pings*. He trusts you. He said he'd not bring any more harm to your village."

I hope I sound more convincing than I feel because I recognize the song being sung outside and it's making my heart hammer with apprehension.

> *Rudolph, the big fat reindeer*
> *Never had any fucking friends*
> *Rudolph was always lonely*
> *And tonight his story ends.*

"They're going to eat Fjorn!" I shout, racing across the living room to the front door. Elias tries to stop me but I shake him off. If the Goblins are outside, then we need to deal with this once and for all. They need to understand that their reign of terror ends now.

There's so much snow on the other side of the door it's hard to push open, but as I do the sight before us makes me cry out in shock.

There's no bloody deer on the doorstep or buildings on fire, it's much more unbelievable than that.

Elias is by my side in a second. "Oh my God," he gasps. "What on earth have they done?"

CHAPTER TWENTY-NINE

ozens, if not hundreds, of Goblins are standing before Elias' cottage holding hammers, screwdrivers, and saws. Their singing is getting louder, their pin-like teeth glinting in the winter light.

And behind them, The Crazy Reindeer Christmas Village has been completely transformed.

"How..." Elias begins but is unable to finish his sentence.

I have no idea how the Goblins have managed it overnight, without us seeing or hearing anything, but every cabin is now newly painted and varnished, each rafter bedecked with garlands of berries and winter foliage. There are even newly planted shrubs surrounding each cabin and studded with twinkling lights.

I pull on my boots and step outside, my feet sinking into the snow, Elias close behind me.

The Goblins part as we approach the cabin beside his and peer through the windows. Inside it looks like something from a Hygge catalog; tartan curtains, newly varnished wooden walls, felt snowflakes hanging against the glass of the window, and a fireplace adorned with holly and ivy.

Candles flicker on every surface and the table is ladened with bowls of winter fruits and spiced nuts.

The Goblins dance around our feet, clasping on to our legs and chattering excitedly, continuing the same tune.

You both better enjoy it
Come see how we prepare!
When we're done fixing your village
Then we'll shit in your hair!

"Shit in my *what?*"

I look at a Goblin and turn away hastily as he flashes me his teeth and a chainsaw.

"You know what?" I say. "Never mind. This is beautiful. Your dirty songs can't ruin it."

Elias tugs at my sleeve. "Look," he whispers.

I follow his gaze to a giant ice-skating rink in the center of the village, surrounded by dozens of fir trees shining with Christmas lights. The street lamps are now gleaming red and working, illuminating the scene in warm amber tones, and little stalls have been set up displaying an array of sumptuous food and drink.

The excitable chatter dies away and in the blink of an eye the Goblins disappear, nothing but waltzing snow at our feet and little footprints to show where they once were.

"How did they do this?" Elias says, turning in a full circle.

"Magic." I'm grinning from ear to ear. "Us Paranormals aren't all bad, you know. So how are you planning on delivering on your side of the bargain with Juppi? Your customers will notice if your Santa is a giant bloodthirsty goat."

Elias can hardly speak, wandering around his village touching everything as if he's expecting it to vanish into thin air.

"He will play the Joulupukki — as in, the original, *mythical* Santa."

Clever. "And how will you keep him from snacking on the guests?"

Elias turns to me and smiles shyly, sweeping my hair away from my face. He plants a kiss on my cheek then holds me tight.

"Don't worry. I have a plan," he says. "Thank you for everything, Saskia. You saved my business."

I kiss him back, then step back. "Elias! *Tell me your plan!*"

He chuckles. "The Goblins will help me make the toys, like back in the olden days. My workers are getting old, they can't keep up with demand, and we know these little creatures are good at making and painting stuff." He signals at the repairs they've managed to do in a matter of hours.

"And the goat?"

He shrugs. "He will stay in the cave, but we are going to make it part of the adult 'Christmas of the past' experience. Something a little more creepy, in keeping with our traditional myths and legends. He's going to give a tour of the Amethyst caves while telling the tale of Finland's original Father of Christmas. No one will know he's the real deal." Elias laughs. "As far as how to make sure he doesn't eat the guests I have some ideas — I either have to hope my elaborate dishes are enough to ward away his taste for blood, or I talk to Kari."

His ex. Right. I forgot about her.

I link arms with him and place my head on his shoulder, and he kisses my crown.

"Time to get word out," he says. "Hullu Poro is back."

CHAPTER THIRTY

"This kitchen is...it's all so amazing," Elias says, kneading rye dough on his brand-new amethyst countertop. Elias has not stopped exclaiming and pointing things out since we left his cabin. It's weird to see him so animated. He towers over me as he holds out a wooden spoon.

"Taste."

I oblige and smile.

"Nettle cream," he explains proudly. Elias has been cooking all day, ever since we woke up and discovered the Goblins had restored his village to its former glory.

Elias is already joyfully reaching out with another thing for me to taste, this time sweet cheese topped with jam. It's weird to see him so animated. I almost miss the old 'get off my lawn' grumpy version. *Almost.*

His hand lingers a little too long on my hips and a moment later his lips are on my neck, enticing me with a fourth course. I shove him playfully.

"Get back to cooking, you've promised the whole village an evening feast."

There's a glint in his eyes as he resumes.

Brand new copper pots gleam over the new stove, his pantry returned to even better than it was before, every shelf stacked with glistening jars of freshly pickled beetroot, radish, and cucumber. Some of them, apparently, pickled by Fjorn who, as it turns out, is a master pickler.

Elias hands me a tray of Rye bread which I carry to the grand hall. The large dining space is warm and inviting now, no sign of its previous doom and gloom, with long tables running along its center complete with chandeliers of real candles and ivy floating above our heads. Everything is so beautiful I've forgotten I'm supposed to be going home in three days.

I sigh. At least I have a killer Santa goat story to go home with, which in turn is bound to drive business for Elias on the Blood Web. I snicker as I imagine a bunch of Paranormals booking rooms at the Hullu Poro to enjoy the goat Santa's show tunes in the flesh. Then I get a little sad because maybe this time next year Elias will be fucking a hot Vamp with candy cane-stained fangs and will have forgotten all about me. Oh well, being here was a pipe dream anyway. Short and sweet. I belong in New York, looking for Mikayla.

Elias's breath is suddenly hot on my skin.

"What are you thinking about?" He kisses me behind the ear.

"What do you think will happen to Walker's village?" I say, although that's not at all what I was thinking about.

Elias' expression sobers. "I'm sure someone else will take it over, some big, fancy company. Or maybe he had heirs."

"Kari would know."

Elias nods and looks concerned again, so I give him a playful nudge to distract him. "Look around. All of this is *way* better than Christmas World. It's fucking amazing."

His smile meets his icy blue eyes.

"Come taste my fresh batch of lingonberry." He takes my hand and leads me back to the kitchen.

"Is that euphemism?"

"What?"

"Never mind."

CHAPTER THIRTY-ONE

Turns out Elias literally wanted me to taste his lingonberry jam. Then we spend another hour running around the resort checking we have everything for the Christmas Day celebration.

I run my hand across the shiny new costumes that hang in the freshly-painted changing room, and grin at the large cupboard full of new props and extra hand-made decorations.

No more DIY last-minute sewing jobs for me to do this time. The Goblins have thought of everything. No wonder Santa made all the little elves his bitch. These tiny Paranormals are so quick and crafty that they could set up the White House for Christmas in under an hour.

"I think we're all set to go," Elias says, slightly out of breath.

"Time to put on that Santa costume," I say, wiggling my brows.

"Not so fast!" booms a voice at the door.

A man with a thick white beard and small specs balanced on the tip of his nose has appeared in the reception area. He stops short at the sight of the elaborately decorated entrance, runs a gloved hand through his thick white hair, and laughs, making his round tummy shake.

"Why, it looks just like the village when I was a young child."

"Father!" Elias cries, running over to him and nearly knocking the old man off his feet.

"My boy," his father says, squeezing his eyes shut as he holds his son to him tightly. Elias' mother appears beside them and holds her hand to her son's cheek, the three of them suspended in a moment in time.

"How?" Elias' father says, his booming voice full of pride, eyes twinkling with tears.

A soft humming can be heard outside. A Christmas tune as if sung by many tiny children.

"I had some help," Elias says, signaling over at me. "I believe Christmas brings its own special magic."

The start of a Goblin carol carries on the air and I hurry to close the door.

Santa baby, slip a finger up Saskia's tree...for me...

Elias and I both cough loudly to cover up the filthy Goblin tune, but it just gets louder.

Mr. Elias, hurry down Saskia's chimney tonight!

Jesus. It's like Samuel L. Jackson carolling! We both cough louder and Elias's mom starts to pat me on the back to help with my choking.

I calm myself down and shake the old man's hand.

"Elias has told us all about you," his father says to me. "Thank you, Saskia, for all of your help," he says, his teary blue eyes identical to that of his son's.

Elias is excited to show them around, and as he points out each new feature in the kitchen and the grand tree in the lobby I fetch us all a glass of salmiakki.

"I'll leave you to it," I say. "I'm going to get ready now."

Elias mouths a 'thank you' and gives me a wink, and my belly burns with a warmth that I'm sure is more than just the salty liquorice liquor.

CHAPTER THIRTY-TWO

Back in my now-sumptuous cabin I shower, in actual hot water, and put on my green crushed velvet dress and boots. I've plaited my hair in the old Finnish style, giving it a modern twist by fashioning a leafy crown from ivy and berries. I look like an old woodland nymph, which is a lot more in keeping with the new-look Christmas village than my previous dancing on the North Pole look.

I can see Elias out of the window showing his parents around the village, all three faces flushed with glee, so I take my time making notes about the story I need to write for the Blood Web and packing up.

I look at the message Jackson sent me this morning. I still haven't replied.

Merry Christmas boss, I hope you're not celebrating with a festive Kitty Kity bang bang. If you are, that's cool, I don't judge. Judge-free Judy, over here.

I have your story. I'll be back in three days.

He responds immediately. Doesn't the man have something better to be doing on Christmas day?

What do mean? What story?

Is he snorting snow? Or is this his idea of a joke?

I don't have the energy to tell him all the details via the Blood Web, he'll get to read my draft soon enough.

I place another sweater in my suitcase, making space by pushing a few books aside and my vibrator, which thanks to Elias has remained unused. I actually bought this bad baby on the Blood Web, it's bewitched to never run out of charge. Maybe I'll leave it for the Juppi, he seems to have a lot of pent-up tension and I'm guessing he'd prefer dildos to pocket pussies. Even though I wouldn't want to assume anything just because his approach to villainy is a little Broadway. What does goat genitalia look like, anyway?

I'm mid-goat-hypothesizing when my fingers close around a package and a card. I turn it over in my hand. The box is perfectly wrapped, complete with a gold ribbon. I turn over the label, instantly recognizing Jackson's handwriting.

A gift? Jackson is not the sentimental type. Why would he sneak a gift into my stuff?

Merry Christmas, Saskia

You have probably worked out by now there was no real assignment. I used the weak lead as an excuse to send you somewhere special for the holidays because it was your first without Mikayla.

I hope you've had lots of fun and soaked up the magic of Christmas without worrying about your family for a few days. You deserve that, Saskia..and a lot more.

Warmest regards

Jackson

I don't know if to laugh or cry.

So, Jackson thought he was doing something *sweet* when he sent me to a Goblin-infested Christmas village in the middle of nowhere?

He really thought it was a dead-end and I'd be spending my time sipping hot chocolate and reading Finnish fables by the fire, instead of watching a goat monster eat a corrupt Texan in a rhinestoned cowboy hat.

I chuckle softly and gaze at the gift in my hand. Silly, silly Jackson. It's...kind of sweet, really. My stomach fills with a soft, gooey sensation like I've eaten too many S'mores.

This is all *very* un-Jackson-like.

I slowly peel away the paper and lift out the gift. It's a snow globe, and inside are two little girls holding hands. They look exactly like Mikayla and I did as children. My throat aches and I wipe away a tear. Mikayla would have loved it here — all we ever wanted as children was a white Christmas. I shake my gift, watching the glittery snow settle over the two little girls beaming up at the sky.

As soon as I find my sister I'm bringing her to Lapland. Because I *will* find her. I will never stop until I do.

I sniff and reply to Jackson's text message. Writing and deleting a million times until I stop sounding as emotional as I feel.

Merry Christmas, boss!

Thank you for both of my gifts.

Let's just say the magic you were hoping I'd enjoy out here got a little more magical than I bargained for. But boy, do I have a story for you. Ever heard of Arctic Goblins?

I'll be home before the New Year.

Saskia x

My phone buzzes immediately but I turn it off. Let him stew on that bit longer, he's not the only one who can pull a Christmas surprise or two.

Now then, I wonder what gift should I bring *him* back? Would a stone Goblin paperweight fit in my carry-on?

CHAPTER THIRTY-THREE

The sound of squeals and giggling outside has my heart shuddering again when I realize it's just the happy cries of children's laughter. I guess Elias and his family have begun the Santa gift-giving.

I slip my duffel coat and scarf over my velvet dress and step outside, laughing out loud at the sight that greets me. Word has clearly got out that The Crazy Reindeer has been rejuvenated back to its former glory and the village is now teeming with families and excitable children.

A woman is strapping on a pair of skates to a little girl's boots. I recognize her as the woman who worked on the amethyst stand at Christmas World. I tap the woman on the shoulder, curious as to what she's doing here.

"Hey, I thought you worked at Christmas World?"

The little girl skates off as the woman stands back up.

"I work here now," she says with a huge grin.

"Oh. And what did your boss have to say about that?"

He's dead. I know Walker's definitely dead, I saw Juppi throw his femur over his shoulder, but I haven't thought about how the goat will have covered up the Texan's disappearance. Goblins are good at DIY but I'm not so sure they're good at PR crisis management.

The woman looks from side to side, clearly nervous to share the latest news.

"It pains me to say this…"

Ping. OK, so she was never Team Texas.

"My old boss, Michael Walker, is dead." She pauses for dramatic effect. No ping. I cover my mouth in the best impression of 'shocked' that I can muster.

"His body was found in the woods last night. The news is saying he was attacked by wolves."

One *ping.*

"Wolves?" I say, doing my best to sound outraged.

"Yes, although we locals, we know the real dangers of those woods. Darkness lies there. Things not of this world." Then she shrugs, like none of it really matters anymore. "Well, he should have been more respectful of our customs."

"What's going to happen to Christmas World?" I ask.

She shrugs again, pushing her hands deep into her anorak.

"My cousin works for the local council and I heard weeks ago that they were going to close down all his villages anyway. He was involved in some kind of embezzlement."

I wait for the pings but she's telling the truth. Well waddayaknow? Even without a little Paranormal help, Elias would have been back on his feet eventually.

"So Elias gave you a job?" I ask.

She beams, her face lighting up.

"You know Elias. So handsome. So kind." She blushes and I look away.

She's right though, Elias is one hunka burnin' Santa.

"Look at this place," the woman continues nostalgically. "It looks just like it did when I was a little girl now everything is up and running again. I heard Elias has already rented out a few rooms for next year. If he keeps going like this, he'll be employing the whole town!"

I stand there open-mouthed. It's been less than twenty-four hours since Elias made a bargain with the Joulupukki. When that goat makes a promise he clearly means it.

I thank the woman for the news, making all the right noises in the right places, quickly hurrying over to the main building where Elias is standing behind reception wearing a Santa hat and a red lumberjack shirt. It's not a combo that normally does it for me, but alongside his stubbly square jaw and ice-blue eyes, I'm ready to be on his naughty list.

His mother and father are in the main hall giving out gifts to children — a much more authentic Mr. and Mrs. Claus than Elias and I ever made.

"Hey," he says, watching me cross the foyer as I unbutton my coat and reveal my festive outfit. His hungry eyes take me in.

"You look beautiful."

"Really? I thought it was the Mrs. Claus outfit that did it for you."

He shakes his head, exasperated. "You and your jokes, Saskia."

Elias steps away from the desk and scoops me down into a dramatic dip, kissing me slowly on the lips. "Mistletoe," he says, nodding up to the beamed ceiling. God, he's gone and put it everywhere.

All this time he's been making references to me being American because of my accent. I don't have the heart to tell him I'm Spanish.

"News of Walker's death reached Christmas World."

Elias nods. "Kari rang me."

"Is she totally devastated?"

Elias makes a sad face. "Maybe. I don't know. Kari loves everyone."

He stands up on his tip-toes and reaches up for the mistletoe. Pinching it between his fingers he holds it in front of me and grins.

"Let's take this with us. I have a few other places I want to kiss you."

I want to ask him if he means geographical places or places on my body, because I would prefer the latter, but we're interrupted by the tinkle of the reception door. Standing in the doorway is Fjorn in his human form wearing actual clothes — he looks so cute in his angora jumper, thick coat and striped scarf. In his mittened hand is another hand, belonging to an equally cute boy.

"Merry Christmas," I say, planting a kiss on his cheek. He blushes and nods long and slow, in his reindeer way.

"And to you. This is Erno, my..." He smiles. "My boyfriend."

The boy gives an equally slow nod and I get it. He's a reindeer Shifter too.

"After last night I realized life's too short," Fjorn says. "Sometimes you have to grab life by the antlers and hold on to what's dear. Or, in our case, rein-deer."

The boy laughs softly at his lame joke, his big brown eyes locked on Fjorn's.

"You have the best sense of humor," Erno says, stroking Fjorns arm. I'm not sure Fjorn has ever made a joke before but whatever tickles this dude's tonsils. I grin at them both as Elias points in the direction of the dining hall.

"You're just in time for the feast."

CHAPTER THIRTY-FOUR

The rest of the day is, what I can only describe, as a perfect Christmas day. We eat and drink and there's no sign of any fluffy Goblins causing havoc. We take time to visit the Juppi in his cave and give him jars of jam and Elias's ancestral silver spoons to keep the Goblins happy. Juppi doesn't have much time for us as he's busy rehearsing his act for the nighttime show. Let's just hope the humans assume he's wearing very authentic prosthetics and that the cave is a really well-made set.

I make a mental note to remind Elias to make a sign listing the experience as 18+ because of the dirty songs.

Elias has totally embraced this new spin on his Christmas village. Kari has even put him in touch with another Brew Witch who moonlights making killer festive cocktails, like Sour Bilberry Martinis that magically fill you with childlike glee, and Salted Toffee Mules that make you want to flirt with your enemies. The handy thing about alcohol magic is that humans can't sense it because they just think they are having a good old-fashioned drunken time. He's also asked her to enchant all the cocktails with Vamp repellent, lest the

Juppi changes his mind about the arrangement and decides to enjoy a meaty snack during the interval.

I'm full after dinner but still found room to sample three magical cocktails, but even they're not enough to make me want to stay in a cave all night.

"Let's make a move," I say to Elias, who is more than happy to leave Juppi to his warbling.

"I haven't given you my Christmas present yet," he says, leading me by the hand out of the cave and towards the woods.

"You have. The stone."

Outside all is quiet, nature muffled by a thick blanket of sparkling snow. It's hard to imagine that just a few days ago I was terrified of what was lurking in this forest, but now it looks like something straight out of a fairy tale dream.

"In that case, I haven't given you my *second* present."

He leads me to a clearing where his sleigh, now freshly painted in reds and green and gold, stands resplendent with thick furs. Chilling in the snow is a bottle of champagne and two flutes.

"No ice buckets needed," he says with a grin, kissing me slowly. I part my lips, his warm tongue slipping into my mouth and making me murmur with pleasure.

"Is this my gift?" I ask. "Champagne in the woods?"

"Not quite," he says, signaling for me to lie back in the thick furs.

I do as I'm told and Elias tucks his mistletoe in my hands.

"Tell me where to kiss you, Saskia," he asks, slowly undoing my coat. His hands wander under my dress as I place the mistletoe on my abdomen. Elias lifts up my dress and kisses my stomach. I push the mistletoe further down and his mouth follows as I swallow down my first moan. Goosebumps prick my skin as I drag the mistletoe a little lower. Elias grazes my pubic bone with his lips then strokes it tauntingly with his tongue.

He follows my hand and the little green bundle of leaves as his mouth moves lower and lower still, my free fingers digging into the fur beneath me.

"What about the party?" I mumble, but I can barely speak. He's already pushed my dress around my waist and my tights all the way down. His tongue is blazing hot against my skin.

"The party can wait," he says, his voice a delicious low rumble between my legs. His calloused thumbs run across my thighs as he cups my behind, arching me forward on to his mouth. I swallow a yelp. The Goblins can't be too far away and the last thing I need is to be serenaded by dirty snow Gremlins right now.

My fists bunch the soft furs beneath me as Elia's tongue moves over my center. Boy, this man really puts the lap in Lapland. I groan, stuffing the furs in my mouth as his tongue moves faster and faster.

"More," I whisper urgently, "More."

This time Elias is the one who obeys me. I moan loudly into the dark cold wood, tired of holding it back.

I never thought my Christmas would end with my nails leaving scratch marks on a bright red sleigh in the middle of the Finnish woods.

But who am I to argue with Santa?

ALSO BY CAEDIS KNIGHT

SIRENS OF LOS ANGELES
VAMPIRES OF MOSCOW
WITCHES OF BARCELONA

Out now on Amazon!

ABOUT THE AUTHORS

Caedis Knight is the pen name of two established fantasy authors, Jacqueline Silvester and N J Simmonds. Silvester began her career in screenwriting and lived all over the world before going on to pen her highly successful YA series *Wunderkids*. Spanish Londoner Simmonds' background was originally in marketing before writing her fantasy series *The Indigo Chronicles*, along with various Manga and her thriller debut, *Good Girls Die Last*. Together they created *Blood Web Chronicles* - their first paranormal romance series set in Europe. Great friends and avid travelers, you can find them whizzing between one another's homes in Germany and the Netherlands, or having Zoom calls to excitedly plot Saskia's next humorous sexy adventure.

Did you enjoy the book? Say hi to Caedis and let her and
your friends know!
Find Caedis on Facebook, Twitter and Instagram!

A NOTE FROM THE AUTHORS

We want to thank all of our readers and the Blood Web family for your endless support. A few years ago when we started our little series, we never thought we would end up with such a loyal and wonderful band of international readers!

We wish you a lot of joy and happiness this festive season. Remember to channel the Juppi and treat yourself like the G.O.A.T that you are. As a little festive thanks we've included exclusive character art by N.J Simmonds. Happy holidays!

CXnight

Printed in Great Britain
by Amazon

16716357R00132